MW00873020

Terror Grips the Beach

A Mickke D Grand Strand Murder Mystery Thriller

A work of fiction

Steve McMillen

OTHER NOVELS

Murder on the Front Nine
Cougars at the Beach
Death on Mt. Pleasant

This book is a work of fiction. Names, characters, places and incidents are either products of the author's imagination or are used fictitiously and are not to be construed as real. Any resemblance to actual events, locales or persons, living or dead, is entirely coincidental.

Copyright © 2019 Steve McMillen
All rights reserved.

IBSN: 9781795269858
Kindle Direct Publishing platform
North Charleston, South Carolina

DEDICATION

This book is dedicated to all of the Mickke D fans whose asking about the next book kept me writing. Also, thanks to my editor who helped me stay on the straight and narrow, and to my wife, Beverly, who kept after me to finish the book.

PROLOGUE

Detective Steve Reynolds of the Lancaster Police Department in Ohio is trekking up Mt. Pleasant, a 250-foot-high sandstone formation, left behind by a glacier during the Ice Age. Tagging along with him is Officer Tom Barrish and Detective Ed Connehey, recently transferred from the Reynoldsburg Police Department. Detective Reynolds had received a tip about a missing person from one of his old high school classmates, Mickke MacCandlish, aka Mickke D, a private investigator from Myrtle Beach, South Carolina.

The missing person, Jake Tracy, is a high school classmate of Reynolds and Mickke D. Jake's secretary reported him missing several days ago. He had told her he was going to climb the mountain after lunch and never returned, she'd said.

Detective Reynolds at 6'2" and 250 pounds is bringing up the rear of the three-man search team. Detective Connehey, ex-Special Forces, is leading the group followed by Officer Barrish. They reach the crest of the mountain and take a little-traveled trail that dead-ends into a large forked tree.

Mickke D had told Reynolds that there is a cave on the other side of the tree. He thinks Jake may have gone up there just to nose around. He also told Reynolds to be careful, that it is one scary place.

Detective Connehey is first over the tree, followed by Barrish and Reynolds. There is nothing visible on the other side except for a ten-foot-wide path, which is blocked about fifty feet away by another large tree, making the path impassable. The men carefully gaze over the edge at the 200-foot drop straight down and at a twenty-foot-high vine-covered rock wall behind them. The three men pretty much take up the entire area of the path. If they had to move in a hurry, they would be in a world of hurt.

Officer Barrish is the first to speak. "I don't see a cave. Are you sure Mickke D said it was here? I don't remember him saying anything about a cave when I helped him over that tree the last time we were here."

Reynolds replies, "Of course not, he had been shot and was completely out of it when you helped him over the tree."

Connehey gives Barrish a hard look. "If he said there's a cave here, then there sure as hell is a cave." Connehey knows Mickke D is also ex-Special Forces.

Reynolds adds, "He said to look behind the vines and to be very careful."

Connehey carefully examines the vine-covered wall. Several of the vines have been cut and he can see that it would be possible to squeeze through to the other side. He turns and addresses his comrades, "Someone get a flashlight ready."

Connehey unleashes a large hunting knife from the sheath strapped to his leg and begins to cut away the vine foliage from the rock wall as Barrish shines his flashlight into the unknown black hole. A pungent smell wafts out to greet the three men, as well as a low growl, a cat-like hiss, and the sound of metal clinking together.

"Oh, my God, that smell is gross, and what was that noise?" Barrish calls out, gasping for air.

"Are there any bobcats around here?" Connehey asks, as all three men slowly back away from the vine-covered wall.

Reynolds immediately makes a call on his cell phone. "This is Reynolds. Get me a forensic team up here on Mt. Pleasant right away. Tell them to drive their vehicle up the trail to the crest and we will meet them there. I also want someone stationed at the foot of the trail leading up here. Don't allow anyone up here until I give you the okay."

As Barrish focuses his light on the black hole, Connehey looks at Reynolds and Barrish. "So, are we going in?"

Again, all three hear the low, spine-tingling growl and hissing sound, as well as a metallic clinking noise. "No, we're going to wait until the forensic team shows up," Reynolds finally answers, as all three men continue to back away from the wall.

Barrish asks, "How are all of us going to share this small ledge? What if whatever is in there decides to come out. Who's first over that tree?"

"Good point." Reynolds gets back on his phone. "This is Reynolds again. Send a couple of guys with a chain saw as well." Then he turns toward Barrish. "I'm going to have that tree cut down and if that thing comes out and we can't kill it, then everyone's on their own. But remember, I do have seniority."

Barrish snickers. "Yea, but remember if that thing comes out, I don't have to outrun it. I only need to outrun you."

Reynolds makes a decision. "All right, let's go back up to the crest and wait for the forensic team and tree cutters to show up."

They wait and listen for a few seconds; however, the cave releases no further sounds. The growl is gone along with the hissing and the sound of metal on metal. The overpowering smell of death remains. They all look at each other as their heart rates quicken. They move promptly back over the tree and on to the crest of Mt. Pleasant.

Conversation is at a bare minimum as they sit on the concrete steps leading to the top of the mountain waiting for the forensic team to show up. Reynolds is thinking to himself, *Mickke D, you were right. That is one scary ass place.*

Reynolds receives a call telling him that the forensic team will be delayed, but the tree cutters are on their way. They show up about twenty minutes later. Reynolds, followed by Barrish and Connehey, shows the two men the tree he wants removed. Reynolds calls down to the police at the foot of the trail and tells them to send someone around to the side of Mt. Pleasant where the tree is located and make sure no one is in harm's way on that side of the mountain. They hear the roar of the chain saw as the men proceed to slice into the tree. Ten minutes later, a cracking noise resonates. The tree begins to lean, but then all hell breaks loose!

Everyone hears a gentle rumbling sound and the ground the men are standing on begins to move. "Holy shit!" Barrish exclaims. The ground around the men starts to shake with much greater force. "Get out of here now! It's an earthquake!" The side of the mountain begins to crumble.

Spine-tingling shrieks and screams come from the direction of the cave. The three men along with the tree cutters scramble away just in time, as that portion of the mountain where the cave and the path were located disappears behind a cloud of dust and debris.

After the dust settles and the rumbling subsides, Reynolds, Barrish, and Connehey slowly and carefully venture back toward the location of the cave. They reach the forked tree, which is now dangling over the side of the mountain supported only by shreds of bark. On the other side of the tree, the path and the vine-covered entrance to the cave are gone; only a rock-strewn debris field remains. The cave is now a sealed tomb.

CHAPTER 1

Detective Sam Concile of the North Myrtle Beach Police Department has her cell phone in hand, contemplating making a call to a local private investigator to help with a couple of her cases.

Her first case is a 35-year-old male who died in a private swimming pool at a local resort on the ocean. The second case is a 29-year-old woman also found dead in another private swimming pool one day later in a different resort along the ocean. The coroner ruled both deaths accidental ODs because both victims had water in their lungs and heroin in their blood. There were no signs of bruising or other forms of a possible struggle. The families of both victims said they were both good swimmers, and both parents said their kids were not taking drugs. The families have asked Detective Concile to refer them to anyone who they might hire to investigate the death of their loved ones. She hesitates. The PI has been a real pain in the ass recently, but he is the only qualified gig in town. She sighs as she makes the call.

After seeing the name come up on my phone, I answer on the first ring. "Detective Concile, nice to hear from you. What do I owe the pleasure? I promise I haven't done anything wrong. Trust me."

"Yeah, right. Trusting you would be like putting the fox in charge of the hen house." She gets right to the point. "I may have a couple of investigative jobs for you. Are you interested?"

"Depends. Fill me in."

She tells me about the two cases. I remember reading about them in the paper. She continues, "The only thing that seems strange to me is that they were both fully clothed and the coroner found only one needle mark on each victim."

"I don't see the problem. Sounds like they both died from drowning after taking drugs. Had they been drinking?"

"They had some alcohol in them but not enough to impair either one of them. Anyway, the families won't accept our conclusion and I thought maybe you could look into it and give them an answer, whether good or bad."

I think for a second or two. "Since it's you, Detective, I will be happy to contact them and see what I can do. Text or email me their information. But remember, since I'm doing this for you, you're going to owe me."

"Don't hold your breath, Mickke D. I think you know me better than that. And don't forget..."

I interrupt. "I know. Contact you if I find out anything." I end the call before she can reply.

Actually, I'm glad for a distraction. An old high school friend of mine is missing back in my home town of Lancaster, Ohio, and I am worried that something bad may have happened to him. I have been pondering about whether I should go back and look into it, but now I'll put that off until I check out Detective Concile's cases.

CHAPTER 2

I receive the information from Sam thirty minutes later, along with the parents' phone numbers. The first victim, identified as Skipper Chucks, was a financial planner from Rockingham, N.C. He was 35 and single. He had not been listed as a missing persons and he was not registered at the Rio Bravo Resort where the body was found floating in the pool by a security guard around midnight.

The second victim was Linda Evans, age 29, from Georgetown, S.C. She was a nurse at the Georgetown Hospital. She was also single and not registered at the Shark Fin Resort where her body was discovered, 24 hours later, floating in the pool around 12:30 a.m. by a resort guest who went for a late-night swim. The police were unable to find any type of a relationship between the two victims.

From experience as an investigative officer with Army JAG while in Special Forces, I know interviewing the family of a deceased child is never easy, no matter how old, especially when they are taken away too soon. The parents never think their child would do anything wrong no matter how the evidence is stacked against them.

My first call is to Earl and Vanessa Chucks, the parents of Skipper who died at the Rio Bravo Resort. Vanessa answers. "Mrs. Chucks, this is Mickke MacCandlish. I'm a private investigator in North Myrtle Beach and you were referred to me by Detective Concile of the North Myrtle Beach Police Department. I am so sorry for your loss."

After a big sigh, she replies, "Mr. MacCandlish, thank you so much and thank you for calling. We want to find out what really happened to our son."

"The way I work, Mrs. Chucks…"

"Oh, please call me Vanessa."

"Okay, Vanessa. You can call me Mickke D. The way I work is I gather some information and do some preliminary work. If I find justification for a further investigation, we can go forward. Is that all right with you?"

"That's fine, but we are willing to pay you up front."

"That's not necessary. Do you mind if I ask you some questions about your son?"

"Go right ahead."

"Was your son married?"

"No, he was divorced. He married Tommie Lu right out of college. He was 23 and she was 20. It lasted about four years. Thank goodness, they never had any children. Divorce is always so hard on the children. He's been single for almost eight years now. He had just turned 35." I can hear grief in her voice.

"Did he have a girlfriend or was he dating anyone?"

"Oh, I'm not sure if he had a steady girlfriend. He really didn't discuss those things with us."

"What exactly did he do as a financial planner?"

"Well, all we knew was that he helped people invest their money. He said he had some very rich clients but he never told us who they were."

"Was he in debt to anyone? Did he have a big mortgage on a home or business?"

"I don't know. He had a big house outside of town and an office in a nice building in town."

Now I ask the tough questions. "Did he have any health issues? Did either of you know he was taking heroin?"

With disdain in her voice, she replies, "Oh, no. Our son was not a drug addict. He was into this holistic health thing. He had a so-called mentor here in town for a while, but for some reason he gave up on her and started going to another person in the Myrtle Beach area. He used to make two trips a month to the beach. Oh, my goodness, maybe that was why he was in Myrtle Beach."

"Did he own a home or condo in Myrtle Beach?"

"Not that I ever knew of."

"Well, thank you, Vanessa. You've been a big help. By the way, does his ex-wife still live in Rockingham, and do you remember the name of his mentor there?" I ask.

"No, Tommie Lu moved away right after the divorce and he never mentioned the name of his mentor." I thank Vanessa again, tell her I will get back to her, and end the call.

I make some notes and then make a call to the parents of Linda Evans. Jim and Candy Evans live in Michigan and Candy answers my call. I again offer my condolences and explain why I am calling. "Do you mind if I ask you some questions about your daughter, Mrs. Evans?"

I can hear her take a deep breath before answering. "Not at all Mr. MacCandlish, and please call me Candy. Jim and I are so glad you called. We will do anything to help you find out what really happened to our daughter. And, we want you to know one thing: our daughter was not on drugs. She was a nurse and despised the thought of people taking illegal drugs."

"How long has your daughter lived in Georgetown?"

"She moved there almost three years ago. She hated the cold and snow up here in Michigan."

"Did she have a steady boyfriend or was she in any kind of a relationship?"

She hesitates before answering. "Well, not that I know of. She did go out with friends but I don't think she was serious about anyone, although she did tell me she had met a nice guy."

"Did she give you the name of her friend?"

"No, she had only met him a couple of days ago."

"Was she in debt to anyone or did she have any large bills?"

"No, I don't think so."

"Did she have any health problems that you know of?"

"Oh no, she was a health nut. She was into holistic medicine. That's why I know she was not taking heroin."

I pause. "Did she have any type of a holistic mentor in Georgetown?"

"No, she was going to someone in the Myrtle Beach area, I think."

"Did she ever mention her mentor's name?"

"No, I don't think so. What does that have to do with her death?"

"I'm not sure, just trying to gather information. I think that's all I need for now. I'll be back to you as soon as I learn something."

"Thank you, Mr. MacCandlish."

After hanging up, I say aloud, "So both of them were into holistic medicine. I guess I had better call Detective Concile."

CHAPTER 3

Sam answers on the first ring. "If you're going to tell me you solved both cases already, I'm going to come over there and shoot your sorry ass."

"I'm good, detective, but I'm not that good. No, I was wondering if you know anyone in the field of holistic medicine in the area."

"And what does holistic medicine have to do with the cases?"

"Maybe nothing, maybe everything. Do you know anyone?"

She ponders the question. "You know what? I think the lady I buy my eggs from is into holistic medicine. She lives in Little River and everyone calls her the crazy chicken lady. I'll text you directions." She laughs. "You two are going to get along just fine."

I'm not sure what she meant by that, but I hang up and go down the hall to Jim Bolin's office. Jim is a retired FBI special agent and my neighbor. He actually runs the private investigation side of my business ventures. I ask him to see if the Bureau has any information on either one of Sam's deceased victims. He tells me he will check with his contacts and let me know.

I receive the directions from Sam, jump into my vehicle, and drive over to the address she texted me. The paved road quickly turns into a dirt road with huge live oak trees lining the way and providing a canopy of shade. I make a sharp "s" curve and turn into the first driveway on the left. It has a large gate surrounded by a chain-link fence. I notice a large NO TRESSPASSING sign on the gate. I see goats, pigs, chickens, and a cow wandering around inside the fenced-in property, along with several boats in all shapes and sizes. I cannot see any sign of a house or building. I locate the monitor on the post next to the gate and push the button. After a few seconds, I push it again. Finally, a woman's voice, sounding rather irritated, answers, "Yes, what can I do for you?"

"Hi, I would like to buy a dozen eggs," I reply.

"They're $4.00 a dozen or two dozen for $7.00. Needs to be cash, don't do plastic."

"I'll take a dozen," I say.

"Do you have the correct amount or do I need to bring change?"

"I've got a five."

"I'll bring you a dollar."

Before I can say anything else, she terminates the conversation.

About five minutes later, I see a person coming down the dirt and gravel lane in jeans, wearing dark sunglasses and a gray hoodie covering her head. She is carrying a plastic bag. Not far behind her are two dogs, one Doberman and one German shepherd. As soon as the dogs observe me, they quickly advance on the closed gate, baring their teeth, barking and growling. The hooded stranger shouts a command and both dogs sit but continue showing me their teeth.

The woman in the hoodie hands me the plastic bag. "I didn't have a dollar in change, so I'm giving you eighteen eggs for $5."

I hand her the five and take the plastic bag. I eye the proximity of the dogs and then say, "Thank you, but I'm also hoping you can answer some questions for me."

Raising her voice and giving me a look to kill, or at least wound and maim, she replies, "I'm sorry, do I look like a librarian to you? Are you here to buy eggs or ask questions? You're new. Who told you about me?"

Still eyeing the dogs, I answer, "Detective Concile of the North Myrtle Beach Police Department told me to look you up. I'm looking for information on holistic medicine?"

Immediately, her posture and demeanor changes. She gives a hand command and the dogs lie down and close their mouths. "Sure, Detective Sam. Nice lady. How can I help you?"

"I'm a private investigator and I'm looking into a case where two people died and they were both into holistic medicine."

A change in composure covers her face. She looks around the premises before answering. "Can we meet somewhere and discuss this later?"

"Sure, you name the place and time."

She contemplates the question. "How about tomorrow morning across the street at Mickey D's, let's say around ten?"

I laugh. "Why are you laughing?" she quips.

"That's my name, Mickke D. Works for me. See you in the morning."

The hooded stranger and her companions turn, walk back up the lane, and disappear in the trees. The dogs bark several times before leaving as if sending me a message.

CHAPTER 4

The following morning I arrive at McDonald's at 9:45. I grab a corner table and watch as people enter and leave the restaurant. At almost exactly ten, a young woman enters. Her features are sharply defined, with large expressive eyes, trim and petite, dressed in a blue knee-length skirt with a low-cut V-neck top. She presents an appealing package just shy of all-out beauty, and she is staring at me. After a few seconds, she waves and walks toward my table.

I find myself jolted back into the past as I casually stand up and wave back. I have always been a sucker for a beautiful woman. That's why I have been married three times, divorced three times, and broke three times. But, right now, none of that seems to matter. I am dumb-founded. Why would this lovely creature be waving at me? Then I remember, the woman yesterday was wearing a hoodie and sunglasses. I never really got a good look at her face. As she gets closer, I begin to see a resemblance to the hooded woman I met yesterday. She extends her hand and plants a strong handshake on me. "We weren't formally introduced yesterday. I'm Jo-Anne Jefferson."

I recognize the voice. "Well, Jo-Anne Jefferson, I'm Mickke D. Are your dogs out in the car?"

"No, they're home, and in case you ever come back, their bark is much worse than their bite, but don't tell anyone."

I'm thinking to myself, "Why is this person who yesterday was pretty much in a pissed off mood all of a sudden so nice to me?"

She must have noticed my confusion. "I called Detective Sam last night and she gave me the low-down on you."

I smile, but inside I'm thinking, *Oh, my God, I can't imagine what Sam may have told her about me.*

I get Jo-Anne a cup of coffee and after some small chitchat, I begin my questions, "So Jo-Anne, what do you do besides raise chickens and sell eggs?"

She looks around the restaurant then whispers, "I'm a mentor for holistic medicine."

I whisper back, "Why are you whispering?"

Continuing her whisper, she replies, "Because I was a mentor to both of those people who were found dead in the swimming pools."

Still somewhat intrigued by this lovely woman, I am completely caught off guard. "Oh, my God, did you tell Detective Concile that?"

She now speaks with only a half-whisper, "Of course not. She didn't ask, and what would that have to do with their deaths? And besides, I didn't want to get involved. Unless our conversation is confidential, I'm done answering questions."

Do I want to piss-off Jo-Anne or Detective Sam? I give her my most trustworthy look and respond, "What's said in Mickey D's stays in Mickey D's."

She half-smiles. "Okay, continue."

"First of all, what exactly is holistic medicine?" I ask.

"Holistic medicine involves a person's physical, emotional, mental, and spiritual health. It uses therapies to treat the whole person, not just their physical symptoms."

"That sounds intriguing. Did Skipper and Linda know each other?"

"Well, I'm not sure. They both had appointments in my office at the same time a few days before they died. I never saw either one of them after that."

"Did either one of them seem troubled or scared in any way?"

"Not at all. They were both happy campers and as healthy as a horse."

After some more small talk and before she leaves, I ask her for her phone number just in case I may have some more questions for her. She hesitates and then laughs as she gives me her business card along with her cell phone number. "Sam said you would probably want my number." She turns and saunters out the door.

As I watch her leave, I am thinking, I will definitely have some more questions for you, young lady.

CHAPTER 5

The moment Skipper Chucks walked into Jo-Anne Jefferson's office, he noticed Linda Evans sitting in the waiting room. He took a seat across from her and picked up a magazine, though the truth be known he was more interested in looking at Linda than reading the magazine. They both smiled at each other.

Skipper, not being a shy guy and noticing she was not sporting a wedding ring, walked across the room and took the chair next to her. They chatted and laughed until the receptionist called Linda's name. Knowing he may only have one shot at this lovely woman, he made his move. "Say, would you like to have a drink after leaving here today?"

She paused, studying his handsome face and dark wavy hair. After not much thought, she agreed, saying she would wait for him outside. After both of their sessions were over, they met and decided to go down by the waterfront and have a drink. They also agreed they would drive separately.

They find a quaint little restaurant on the waterway and sit down next to a window with a view of the marina. It's too early for happy hour and they are the only customers in the restaurant. While sipping on a cold drink, they notice a fishing boat enter the marina. After docking, two men in suits, which is strange to see at the beach, climb onboard. One of the deckhands moves some fish and holds up a white plastic bag. They notice one of the suits gestures at him to put it down.

Behind Skipper and Linda, their waiter, Mike Keegan, watches and hears Skipper say in almost a whisper, "Was that cocaine?"

Mike immediately leaves the restaurant and rushes out to the boat. He whispers to one of the suits. They both look up toward the window where the couple was seated and only half-full glasses remain. The suit says something to Mr. Keegan.

Skipper and Linda are going out the front entrance as the waiter re-enters through the back door. She gives Skipper her cell phone number and they leave in their separate vehicles. They decide not to call the police because neither one of them wants to get involved.

Mike follows them at a respectable distance and takes cell phone pictures of both of their license plates. He also finds and writes down the name on the credit card used to pay their bar bill.

The man in the suit waits until Mike returns with the information on their peeping toms. He now has Skipper's name and both of their license plates. He hands the waiter a $100 dollar bill and thanks him. He motions to the other suit. "See to it that the deckhand who held up the sugar does not return from the next run. We can't afford screw-ups like this."

Suit 2 nods. He calls the captain of the boat over, and orders him to eliminate the deck hand on the next run. He then moves back to Suit 1 and gives him a thumbs up. They normally wait until after dark to unload their contraband but they decide to move the boat immediately to a less conspicuous location and to unload their "sugar" immediately.

Suit 1 says to 2, "When we get back to the office, find those two people and get rid of them. The sooner the better, and make it look like an accident."

CHAPTER 6

I decide to go to the library to pick up some reading material on holistic medicine, as well as some fictional novels. I want to research holistic medicine, just in case I need to call Jo-Anne Jefferson again.

I'm seated in the local library, trying to determine which of the three books I have with me, I'm going to check out. If I take all three, I'll never read them before the return dates. I have a non-fiction book on holistic medicine and two fiction novels. I always read the jacket, leaf through the book to make sure the print is not too small, and finally I read the first paragraph of the book. If it doesn't get my attention, I move on to the next one.

I'm leafing through my second choice and I notice a torn folded napkin placed between two of the pages. Out of curiosity, I open the napkin and find a scribbled note: Please help me, I think they're going to kill me. There is no name or date, just a call for help or a prank placed there by some kids who do not like spending time at the library.

If I was a smart man, I would just close the book and move on to the next one, but the PI in me says don't you dare. I look around the room to see if anyone is watching me, but no one catches my eye as a possible threat. So now what do I do? Call Detective Concile and have her laugh at me, or see what I can find out on my own?

I casually walk around the library and see if anyone looks stressed, worried or anxious. Everyone looks happy and content. Next, I walk up to the desk. A young woman asks if she can help me. With my best smile and gazing at her nametag, I reply, "Well, Sherry, I sure hope so. Would it be possible for you to tell me who checked this book out last?"

Sherry gets a funny look on her face and before she can say no, I pull a staged twenty-dollar bill out of the middle of the book. "I found this twenty in the book and I'm going to guess the person reading it was using it as a bookmark. I would just like to make sure it gets back to the right person." I flash my PI license and a big smile and continue, "Can you help me?"

With a puzzled look, she takes the book, goes over to her computer, starts pushing keys and writes something down on a notepad. She returns with the note and a flirtatious wink. "This did not come from me."

I nod my head, take the note, and leave. I look at the note once I'm in my vehicle. The name is Mary Kay Henderson and she lives in Cherry Grove. There is an address but no phone number. Since I'm close, I opt to drive by the address, which seems to be an apartment complex. As I turn into the complex, I notice police cars and an EMT unit. I walk slowly up to where everyone is congregated, and low and behold, there is my favorite detective, Sam Concile.

She turns just as I get close and gets that look on her face. "What the hell are you doing here?" she calls out.

"Well, nice to see you too, detective. What's going on?"

"Robbery gone bad. Young girl in her twenties, stabbed to death. Again, why are you here?"

"Was her name Mary Kay Henderson?"

"Mickke D, you never cease to amaze me. How did you know that?"

I pull the torn napkin from my pocket and hand it to her. “I found this in a library book about thirty minutes ago. I checked on who last borrowed the book and it was Mary Kay Henderson at this address.”

CHAPTER 7

Jeffrey Barrons wears a coat and tie to work every day. He owns and operates a company that manages condo associations along the Grand Strand of South Carolina. He is originally from Colombia by way of New York City. He has been in the area for two years. He moved here with several key people to set up the condo management company and a drug smuggling business based in the Myrtle Beach area. His employees do a great job managing condos along the beach but have no idea what upper management does on the side.

Jeffrey moves drugs from South America and Mexico into Myrtle Beach and then distributes them all over the Southeast. He has an elaborate distribution team that moves drugs into the country one day and leaves the beach the next day. He never touches the drugs and none of the drugs are distributed in Myrtle Beach. His only job is to see that he gets what he paid for, that the drugs go out the next day, and that no one gets in the way. He considers himself strictly a businessman.

Mary Kay Henderson is the broker in charge of his condo association business, Condo Enterprises, LLC, and she has been with him since he opened the doors. One afternoon as she steps outside the back door for a smoke break, she accidently overhears Jeffery and his right-hand man, Bob Linde talking about how he did away with two people who noticed them with cocaine along the waterfront in Little River. In her rush to go back into the office, she knocks over a large plant, stumbles over the step and falls just as Jeffery and Bob come around the back of the office. "Are you all right, Mary Kay?" Jeffrey asks.

She gets back on her feet and replies, "Oh, I'm fine. I just tripped coming out the door for a smoke break. Thanks for asking."

Jeffrey looks suspiciously at Bob. "So you just came out?"

Nervously, she replies, "Yes sir, thought I would get a quick smoke."

"Are you sure you're okay?" Jeffrey asks with a look on his face Mary Kay has never seen before.

"Oh no, I'm fine."

"Let me know if you need anything, okay?"

Mary Kay nods and quickly returns to her office forgetting about the smoke break. She is scared and has no idea what she should do. Do Jeffrey and Bob think she heard their conversation? Was she imagining the reference to cocaine? Should she call the police? She carefully sneaks a look out her office window and sees Jeffrey and Bob in a heated discussion in the parking lot and she can tell Jeffrey is very adamant about something.

As confusion and desperation set in, she hurriedly scribbles a note on a napkin and places it in a library book she is planning to return. In her befuddled state, she forgets to sign the note. She walks out to her secretary and asks her to drop off the book on her way home because she knows the girl goes right by the library. She leaves the office and goes directly home to decide what her next move will be. After a couple glasses of wine, she decides not to jump to any conclusions. She will return to work tomorrow as if nothing happened.

CHAPTER 8

Jeffrey and Bob have other plans for Mary Kay "I think she heard us talking. Get rid of her just like the other two," Jeffrey says.

"Are you sure?" Bob asks.

"Yes, I'm sure. I noticed a cigarette lying on the ground, which had just been put out. She couldn't have smoked it that fast if she had just come outside. Do you have a problem with that?"

"No sir, I'm just a little concerned that three people dying the same way may set off the possibility that maybe those other two were not just an unfortunate overdose."

"Well, then kill her any way you want. Just do it."

As Bob turns to leave, Jeffrey receives a text message. "Hold on a minute Bob, listen to this. This text is from a member of the Valdez family back in Colombia. They used to be a client of mine." He reads the text. Understand you're in Myrtle Beach, South Carolina. I need someone removed up there. I'll pay $100,000.00 to have the job done. Are you interested?

"Wow, are you going to take the contract?" Bob quickly asks.

"Probably not, but if you want to do it, I'll let them know."

"Sure, I'll do it. Have them send me the particulars."

Jeffrey returns the text and tells them that he will accept the contract and to send the details.

CHAPTER 9

After a two-hour meeting with the mayor and the police chief, Detective Reynolds is told that because of the possibility of a major landslide, the cave will not be excavated. It is just too dangerous. The whole side of Mt. Pleasant could come down. The police chief also tells him in private that it would be a good idea not to mention anything about strange sounds coming from the cave. Detective Reynolds reluctantly agrees; however, he does ask what he should do about Jake. The chief tells him to find some hard evidence that Jake was in the cave. If he can't, then treat him as a missing persons case and look elsewhere.

Reynolds leaves the meeting not a happy camper. He keeps pondering the thought that maybe they should have gone in and searched the cave for Jake. He also thinks about the fact that if all three of them had been inside when the rumbling began, they would all be dead or entombed in the cave.

He returns to his office and tells Barrish and Connehey about the decision. Both of them feel the same way. Maybe they should have gone in but it's too late now to second-guess. Reynolds also tells them not to mention anything about the strange sounds they heard coming from the cave. Both men nod their heads in agreement.

Reynolds knows he should call Mickke D and give him the news.

*****

I answer on the first ring. “Hey, big Steve. Did you find anything out about Jake?”

He gives me the entire gruesome details of their search, including what happened on Mt. Pleasant. I am not sure what to say. “Thanks Steve, I never should have told Jake about the cave.”

“Listen, Mickke D, we are not sure he was in there. He may turn up sooner or later.”

“So what do you think set off the landslide? An earthquake?”

“We have no idea. The only damage was right there where the cave was located.”

“Thanks again for the update. I may make a trip up and see what I can find out.”

“You would just be wasting your time. It’s over. I’ll keep you advised of any new developments.”

Without commenting further, I hang up and contemplate not whether to head north, but when to head north.

CHAPTER 10

The day after meeting Detective Concile at the apartment of Mary Kay Henderson, Jim comes into my office and tells me there is not much out there on my two victims. Skipper Chucks seems clean as a whistle except for testifying against one of his clients in federal court about three years ago. A jury found his client guilty and sentenced him to three years in federal prison. Linda Evans is also pretty vanilla except for the fact that her uncle has ties to the Italian mafia.

"Thanks, Jim. Do you know the name of the person who went to federal prison and the name of Linda Evans uncle? Do me one more favor and see what you can find out about a Mary Kay Henderson, who died in a robbery yesterday in North Myrtle Beach."

"No problem. The man who went to prison was Ray Chrystal and Miss Evans uncle is Don Emery. Is this a rush job?"

"No, not really. Can you check on Mr. Chrystal and Mr. Emery as well? I'm going to call Detective Concile and see what she will tell me and then we'll compare notes."

Later that afternoon, I call Detective Concile. "So, detective, have you found out anything about Mary Kay Henderson and maybe why someone would want to rob her and then kill her?"

She hesitates. "And why should I tell you what I found out?"

"Because you owe me one," I quickly reply.

She pauses again. "Okay, but then we are even."

"I'm good with that."

"Well, actually we didn't find out much of anything. We interviewed her boss, co-workers, and neighbors. Everyone liked her."

"So, where did she work? What is her boss's name?"

"She was the office manager and broker in charge, for Condo Enterprises, LLC. Her boss was a Mr. Jeffrey Barrons."

"Thanks, detective, I'll let you know if I find out anything."

"Mickke D, do not interfere with my investigation."

I hang up before replying to her.

I venture over to Jim's office and surprisingly find him there. It's a beautiful day so I figured he would be on the golf course. "Not playing golf this afternoon?"

"No, I think I'll hit the driving range on the way home. What do you need?"

"Along with Mary Kay Henderson, Mr. Emery and Ray Chrystal, can you run a check on Condo Enterprises, LLC, and a guy named Jeffrey Barrons?"

"That's going to take some time. Sure hope you don't need it today?"

"No, tomorrow will be fine."

"No problem, if my guy's in I'll have it for you by the end of the day tomorrow."

I decide not to wait on Jim. Something about this whole thing is beginning to smell. I search for Condo Enterprises on Google and get the address. It's located in North Myrtle Beach, not far away.

Fifteen minutes later, I walk in the front door and ask for Mr. Barrons. A young lady with puffy eyes, probably a close friend of Mary Kay's, asks what this is about. I hand her my card. She disappears down the hall and returns with, I'm guessing, Mr. Barrons, who is followed by another man. Both men are dressed in suits.

"I'm Jeffrey Barrons, Mister..." gazing at my card, "MacCandlish. How can I help you?"

"I wanted to ask you some questions about a current case I'm working on."

"Certainly. Let's go in the conference room. This is an associate of mine, Mr. Linde."

I shake hands with both men and don't like the fact that Mr. Linde is closing the door to the room. Both men have an accent that doesn't go along with their American names, which is giving me cold chills. "I take it you gentlemen are not originally from here?"

Jeffrey answers. "As a matter of fact, you are right. We are from Colombia. Have you ever visited our lovely country, Mr. MacCandlish?"

I am now on full alert. "Yes, as a matter of fact, I have been there several times. Beautiful place."

Just as the temperature and tension in the room begins to soar, my phone rings. I look at the number and say, "Excuse me, gentlemen, I need to take this," and quickly leave the room. The call is from Dr. Horton's office, my dentist, to confirm an appointment, but it came at just the right time. I pop my head back in the room. "Sorry guys that was a 911 call. I have a fire to put out. I hope we can continue this conversation at a later date."

"Come back anytime, Mr. MacCandlish. Mary Kay was a close friend of ours."

I give him a funny look and wave my hand. As I'm leaving the office, I'm thinking, I don't remember mentioning Mary Kay at any point in our conversation. I don't fully relax until I reach my vehicle.

After Mickke D leaves the conference room and after closing the door, Linde looks at Barrons. "He doesn't look that tough to me."

"Just remember, looks can be deceiving. It sure was nice of him to make an appearance so we could check him out. Did you notice he was armed?"

"Yeah, I saw that." Linde replies.

Mr. Barrons and Mr. Linde had just received a dossier pertaining to the "hit" contract from Colombia minutes before Mickke D arrived.

CHAPTER 11

Around 11:30 the next day, Jim comes into my office and takes a seat across from me, which means he has more than just a quick answer to my request. "Well, Mary Kay Henderson was a straight shooter. No problems with her. Mr. Emery fled the States after called upon to testify in a possible fraud case in New York City. Miss Evans was interviewed, but nothing ever came of it. Ray Chrystal is still in Club Med Federal Prison, and Mr. Chucks was never implicated in any wrongdoing. I don't see any connection there. Condo Enterprises, LLC has a good rating and no red flags seem to be flying in that direction."

I can't wait to interject. "Now you're going to give me the bad news, right? You found some problems with Mr. Barrons, didn't you?"

"You smart ass, how did you know that?"

I chuckle, "I went down there yesterday afternoon and left in a hurry. What did you find out?"

"Well, nothing on his name, but when I ran his photo from his South Carolina driver's license, it seems as if the DEA is looking for him. They were watching him in New York but he flew the coop and has been on a most wanted persons watch list ever since."

"How in the world did you get his South Carolina photo?"

"You really don't want to know. Just continue paying my expense account."

I shake my head. "So why does the DEA want him?"

With a smirk on his face, he answers, "You mean you don't already know?"

"I'm going to guess it has something to do with drugs and Colombia."

"Right again. Seems they think he was running drugs from South America to the States. Do you think he knows your friends the Valdez family?"

"I think it's a good possibility. I felt bad vibes in that office. I think we should both be on our toes from now on. If you see Mark before I do, tell him to stay alert as well."

Mark is in charge of my landscape business and is married to Jannie, my receptionist. He is also ex-Special Forces and spent time with me in Colombia.

"By the way, he introduced me to another guy as well, a Mr. Linde. Check on him as well."

"Got a first name?"

I pick up the phone and call the condo office. A woman answers. "Yes, is Tom Linde in please?" I ask.

"Oh, you mean Bob Linde?"

"Yes, thank you. Oh, sorry, I have another call. I'll call right back." I hang up, look at Jim and smile. "His first name is Bob."

"Smart ass," he mutters as he leaves my office, closing the door behind him.

After a few minutes of reflection, I figure it's time to call my favorite detective and bring her up to speed on what I found out. She answers as if she is having a bad day. "Mickke D, now what?"

"I'm just following orders and bringing you up to date. Is this a bad time?"

"Every day's a bad time, but go ahead, enlighten me."

"Okay, did you run any kind of a check on Mr. Barrons over at Condo Enterprises?"

"Of course not, why would I?"

"Well, we did and there could be a possibility the DEA is looking for him."

Silence on the other end. "I did notice he had an accent not from around here."

"That accent is Colombian, south of the border."

"Whoa. Is he looking for you?" She knows about several attacks on me from Colombian assassins.

"I don't think so. I met him and another guy from Colombia named Bob Linde yesterday and no one shot me. You may want to check with DEA and see if they're interested in them."

In as much of an apologetic tone as she can muster, Sam replies, "I'll do that and get back to you. Thanks for the tip."

CHAPTER 12

The following morning around ten, Jannie calls me, "There's a lady out here who said a Detective Concile sent her over to see you." Then she whispers, "She's carrying a gun."

I return her whisper with a whisper of my own, "Thanks Jannie, send her back."

In a minute or so, a stunning woman dressed in jeans, boots, a white blouse and a weapon holstered to her shapely hip illuminates my doorway. As usual, I am at a loss for words. Finally, I stand up and say, "Please come in. What do I owe the pleasure?"

She reaches into her back pocket and pulls out a badge and ID. "Special Agent Karol Colder, DEA. That's Karol with a K. You must be Mickke D. I've heard quite a bit about you."

Why in the world do all of these gorgeous women have to get a report on me from Detective Concile. I just stare at her and probably look like a fool. Finally, I respond, "Have a seat, Agent Colder. How can I help you?"

"Well, Detective Concile called our office and said you may have met someone who could be a person of interest. I just wanted to ask you some questions."

"No problem. Ask away."

She takes a small pad and a pen from her other back pocket and begins. "Why do you think this person may be on our list as a person of interest?"

"I am not about to divulge my sources, but I do believe there is a good chance you may be looking for him."

"And what is this person's name?" she asks.

"His name here is Jeffrey Barrons, however, I think he is from Colombia, South America, by way of New York City and very possibly a drug dealer. He owns Condo Enterprises, LLC in North Myrtle Beach, which manages POAs and HOAs here on the beach. I figure Condo Enterprises is a front for his drug business."

"How and why did you meet him?"

I go into scant details about my investigations into Skipper Chucks, Linda Evans, and Mary Kay Henderson. She makes some notes and then abruptly stands up. "I would like to meet this man. Do you think you can arrange it?"

"Well, I suppose so. Will he recognize you?" I ask.

"If it's the guy I think it is, he has never seen me."

"And if it's another guy who may have met you?"

She gives me a sly grin. "Do you carry a weapon, Mr. MacCandlish?"

"Sometimes." I reply.

"Well, take it along. You may need it. Can you set up a meeting?"

"No problem. What is your cover?"

"I'm just an investigator on your staff."

"Okay, let me call right now." I call Condo Enterprises and get the receptionist I met the other day. She informs me Mr. Barrons is out of town and won't be back until next week. She tells me to call back Tuesday to set up an appointment.

I convey the phone conversation to Agent Colder and we decide to meet here at my office Tuesday morning around ten. Just as she is about to leave, Jim comes barging into my office. "Oh, sorry boss. I have that information you were looking for on..."

I interrupt him before he can say a name. "No problem, Jim. We can discuss that later. This is Agent Colder with the DEA."

He grins and shakes her hand. "Nice to meet you, Agent Colder. Mickke D, we'll talk later."

Jim exits the room and Agent Colder gives me a funny look. "Is he one of your sources, Mr. MacCandlish?"

"Oh no, he was looking into a place for us to play golf this weekend."

She smiles. "I'll see you Tuesday morning, Mickke D. "By the way. Cute name."

After Agent Colder leaves, I sit at my desk and contemplate my next move, and it's not related to the case I'm presently working. I recently got back together, sort of, with my old girlfriend Beverly, a paid assassin with a CIA splinter group. Now, I have met two lovely women within the last few days who I would like to know better. Two of the three women carry a gun, and I'm going to bet the third knows how to use one.

I walk over to the window and watch as Agent Colder walks over to her vehicle, a black Ford sedan. I wonder when the Feds will figure out that you can spot a government agent a mile away just by the car they drive? I just know that she knows I am watching her.

I stop staring out the window and call Jim to tell him I'm on my way to his office. Once I arrive, I ask, "So, what did you find out about Bob Linde?"

"Wow, that DEA agent was hot. What was her name?"

"Jim, focus. Bob Linde?"

"Oh yeah. I can't find out anything on him. My contact with the Bureau came up empty."

"Did you do the DMV thing as well?"

"Yeah, sent the photo and still nothing."

"Okay, keep me informed."

I leave Jim's office and start down the hallway when I hear my name called, "Mickke D." I turn and see Jim motion me back to his office. Once inside, he closes the door and hands me his cell phone. "You need to read this."

I look at the text. Jim. Thought I would give you a heads up. Homeland Security has intercepted some cell phone chatter, which leads them to believe there is a possible terrorist threat over the Fourth of July in Myrtle Beach. They can use all the eyes and ears available in the area. I'll send you details.

"Jim, find Mark and let's have a meeting in my office right away." I look at my watch. It is 11 a.m. July 1, two days before the start of the long holiday weekend.

CHAPTER 13

"**Guys, as** we all know, Myrtle Beach is a large tourist area. On any given weekend during the summer, there could be as many as 200,000 to 300,000 tourists in town. On Fourth of July weekend, there may be 400,000 people in town. So, how in the world is anyone going to find a terrorist with that many people around?"

"Well, one thing is for sure," Mark answers, "If it's a bomb threat, and they're on the beach, it will be the person in a long trench coat. You can't hide a bomb in a bikini."

"You're right, Mark, but that would be the best place to set off a bomb, if it is a bomb threat, wouldn't it?" I reply. "Therefore, this means they would have to carry the explosives in some manner to the beach."

Jim jumps in. "Can the cities and towns along the beach ban coolers over the Fourth of July?"

I answer, "Well, I suppose they could, they banned tents for a while, but I don't think it would get them many brownie points, and how would they explain it without causing a mass panic exodus?" I put my feet up on my desk. "Let me call Detective Concile and find out what she knows. Jim, call me the minute you get more details."

Jim and Mark leave my office as I dial Sam's number. She answers on the second ring. "Well, Mickke D, how did you like Agent Colder?"

"She was great. I have a question for you. Have you been contacted by Homeland Security?"

Silence abounds from her end of the line. Finally, she replies, "I have no idea what you're talking about."

"Detective, it's me. You know damn well what I'm talking about. I have my sources. Do you want some help with this matter or not?"

Again silence and then, "All right, but I don't want to discuss it on the phone. Come down to my office."

"I'll be there in twenty minutes," I reply.

I update Jim and leave the office.

CHAPTER 14

Beverly Beery, Mickke D's on-again off-again girlfriend is back in Atlanta waiting on her next assignment. Her job is to locate and terminate, if necessary. She works for a rogue splinter group of the CIA and reports to Liz Woodkark, aka GG.

Liz is an employee with the Justice Department in Washington, D.C., however that is only a cover. Her real job is to run a rogue cell operation for the CIA around the world. She receives funds through materials confiscated from drug dealers and other wanted persons. Taxpayer money does not subsidize any of her projects. There is no money trail back to her or the group.

GG also received a memo about the possible terror threat in Myrtle Beach. She knows Beverly has a connection in Myrtle Beach, so she contacts her and asks her to immediately go to the beach and see if she can help, but to be careful. Beverly readily accepts and gets on the first flight she can find. She is looking forward to hooking up with Mickke D again, even though theirs is sort of a love-hate relationship.

Once she arrives in town, she checks into the Sleep Inn located next to Harborview Golf Complex, just a hop, skip and a jump from Mickke D's house in River Hills. She considered showing up on his doorstep but decided that probably would not be a good idea. He may shoot her.

CHAPTER 15

I arrive at police headquarters and I am ushered into Detective Concile's office immediately. She gets right to the point. "Okay, so what do you know?"

I look at her and answer, "That there's a possibility of a terror attack this weekend."

She nods her head. "You're right, and we do need some help. Since you're not law enforcement, I can't let you into any meetings. Who is available to help you?"

"Jim Bolen and Mark Yale from my office."

"I know Jim but not Mark."

"Mark is ex-Special Forces and ready to help."

"Okay. I am going to contact Agent Colder and see if she is available."

I smile. "That won't upset me."

"I figured as much, but since she is law enforcement, she'll be in charge of your group."

I hesitate. "Look, detective, we like to do things our own way. She may hinder our style."

"Yeah, I know your style. You'll just have to work that out with her."

"Okay, we'll worry about that later. How can we help?"

She begins, "Here's our plan of action. I want two armed personnel at every beach access location from Cherry Grove all the way to Myrtle Beach. You will be dressed in beach attire and armed with a concealed weapon. Each access location will have security from 9 a.m. to 4 p.m. Saturday through Monday. Everyone will have a police radio, and each team leader will check in every 30 minutes with me. Everyone will be wearing a black wristband that shows you're part of the task force, in case we need to converge on a location."

She pauses to catch her breath and then continues, "I want you and your team to take the first two beach access locations starting at the point in Cherry Grove and coming south. We are looking for anyone who looks like a suspect and is carrying any type of a cooler or object that could hold a bomb, or a weapon. You can take turns walking between access points. If anyone leaves a cooler or object and walks away, I want to know about it. If they do not return within a short time, call and I'll send a cop with a bomb-sniffing dog over. Do not try to disarm anything yourselves. You will take along sandwiches and water in your own cooler, which we will provide. Each cooler will have a large black dot on it. This will be another way to identify you as a member of the task force. Bathroom breaks should be as short as possible. Whatever you do, don't start a stampede or panic at the beach. Any questions?"

"Sounds like three days of fun at the beach. What if it rains?"

"You can leave when everyone on the beach leaves. Make sure no one has left anything behind. Keep an eye out from your vehicle. I don't believe they would try anything unless the beach is crowded."

"Do we have any idea who they are?"

"Not yet, but Homeland Security is working on it."

CHAPTER 16

I return to the office and meet again with Mark and Jim. As I am going over what Detective Sam told me, I get a call from Agent Colder. I push the speaker button on my phone. "Hey, Mickke D, looks like we're going to be working together over the holiday weekend."

"Looks that way. Meet me here in my office Saturday morning at 8:30. We need to be on the beach by nine. Don't forget to wear swim attire and bring a weapon."

"No problem," she replies, "But who put you in charge? Detective Concile said DEA was to take the lead on this."

While smiling at Jim and Mark I say, "That's all fine and dandy Agent Colder, but you still need to be in the office Saturday morning at 8:30. We'll discuss chain of command then."

Agent Colder ends the conversation abruptly. I look at Jim and Mark. "I guess that means she'll be here Saturday morning."

Jim grins, "Since you said we will be working in teams of two, do you want me to work with Agent Colder?"

I grin back, "No, Jim, I'll work with Agent Colder. You and Mark will be a team. Anyway, I thought you had a thing for that new girl working for TC, isn't her name Glenda?"

"I figured that was the way it was going to be, but I thought I would try. Yes, I have been out with Glenda several times. Lovely girl."

Mark quirks, "Oh, come on Jim. We'll have fun at the beach. Remember all the fun we had in Colombia?"

Jim laughs. "Right. I can hardly wait."

CHAPTER 17

Saturday morning, the three of us are gazing out the windows in my office awaiting the arrival of Agent Colder. We watch low-hanging gray clouds disappear and replaced by a translucent morning sky just as Agent Colder pulls into the office parking lot right on time.

She exits her vehicle as the sun peeks through the few remaining clouds. "Look, she brought the sunshine with her," Jim says. Mark and I just shake our heads, but inside I'm agreeing with him.

She is wearing sandals and a beach cover-up, which hangs just above her knees. If she has a weapon, it is not apparent. As she confidently enters my office, I remark, "Agent Colder, I think you already met Jim. This is Mark Yale. I just received a call from Detective Concile and we are good to go. It's going to be a great beach day."

"Great, looking forward to it." She shakes hands firmly with Jim and Mark. "What qualifications do you two have for this mission?"

Before Jim or Mark can answer, I jump in. "Jim is ex-FBI and Mark is ex-Special Forces. Both have been there, done that. Any other questions?"

"Not right now. Always like to know who I'm going into battle with."

I nod. "So Agent Colder, here is your black wristband showing you're part of the task force, and here is your radio. Detective Concile wants us to check in every 30 minutes. Since you're DEA, I guess that's your responsibility. Our locations are the first two beach access points in Cherry

Grove. You and I will take the northern most access point and Jim and Mark will have the next access south. Mark's wife Jannie made some sandwiches for our coolers that Sam sent over, along with soft drinks and water. Do you have any special dietary needs or special drinks?"

"No, that works for me. Are we ready to go? Do you want me to drive?"

"No. The bad guys would spot your vehicle a mile away. We'll take my vehicle, and Jim and Mark will come a few minutes later in a second one."

"Do you have beach chairs, sunscreen, and an umbrella?" I ask Jim.

"Yes, we're set."

"Okay, we'll see you at the beach. Let's have fun in the sun and keep our eyes open."

CHAPTER 18

Jeffrey Barrons is out of town until Sunday, but Bob Linde is not. He has chosen to collect his $100,000 as soon as possible. He finds the location of Mickke D's office and is in the parking lot next door early Saturday morning to see if there is any activity at the office. He watches as Mark and Jim enter the office, followed soon after by Mickke D. Fifteen minutes later, a woman in beach attire arrives in what looks like a law enforcement vehicle and enters the office. They all leave 20 minutes later with coolers and enter two different vehicles.

Linde is confused. They look like they're ready to spend the day at the beach. Regardless, four people are three too many for him to attack. He trails them at a discreet distance and follows them to Cherry Grove Point. He watches as Mickke D and the woman go to one beach access and the other two go to another one. He realizes they must be on a case and leaves the area.

CHAPTER 19

We arrive at our assigned locations and set up shop. Cherry Grove Point is a beautiful beach location. At low tide, there is possibly a quarter-mile of beach to explore. At the very end, or point, is a swash, which goes back into the salt marsh. Many people fish this area. Across from the swash is an island where visitors and locals take their boats to have picnics and relax.

The beauty of the area mesmerizes Agent Colder and after we set up, she goes for a walk. I brought along several of those library books to read and I empty them from my backpack along with my phone. I call Jim and Mark to make sure they are in place. Jim asks, "Hey, did you notice a black SUV that followed us from the office? He parked about a block away and after we headed to the beach, he left. I didn't get a license plate number."

"No, I didn't. Keep your eyes open. We may have more enemies than just terrorists."

"Roger that."

Next, I call Detective Concile and let her know we are ready and that Agent Colder will be giving her the 30-minute updates.

Her only reply is, "Play nice, Mickke D, play nice."

"No problem, detective, no problem."

Agent Colder returns in about fifteen minutes with a big grin on her face. "What a beautiful place. I could probably live here."

"I have a real estate office in my building. I can take care of that for you."

"I'll just bet you could, but I don't think my boyfriend would like the idea of me moving to the beach. We share a great place on Lake Norman, just north of Charlotte."

She just took the wind out of my sails. Well, I guess I can eliminate this young lady from my woman dilemma. Sounds as if she is in a good relationship and she is letting me know as much. Oh well, you win some, and you lose some. It will be all business from here on out.

We settle in, and Agent Colder makes her first radio check at 9:30. Everything is quiet so far along the beach, but it is starting to get busy. Agent Colder is located on my left, closest to the access path. It doesn't take long to figure out she has at least one bad habit. Every time she ends a sentence, she hits me in the arm. Finally, I sternly say, "Agent Colder, if you hit me one more time, I'm going to pick you up and dump you in the ocean."

She gives me a funny look, wondering if I would really do that. "Sorry, bad habit. I have three older brothers, and as kids, we always did that. So, what books are you reading?"

"Oh, I got these at the library the other day. Three murder mysteries by some local author and a book on holistic medicine. A girl at the library told me the murder mysteries were very good. Would you like to read one?"

"Sure, what are my choices?"

"Well, you can read the one on holistic medicine or *Murder on the Front Nine, Cougars at the Beach* or *Death on Mt. Pleasant.*"

"I'll take *Cougars at the Beach.*"

"Does that mean your boyfriend is younger than you?"

"No, it means I'm just not into holistic medicine, golf and mountains."

We read a while, make radio checks, have lunch, and take turns walking between access points looking for anything suspicious. Mark and Jim do the same. Actually, spending this much time at the beach is rather boring, but I guess we could have a worse stakeout location.

Occasionally, a nice-looking, well-built young lady walks by in a skimpy bikini and smiles at me, which perks me up. Agent Colder just snickers. "Come on, Mickke D, give me a break. Those aren't real."

I smile. "And your point is?"

The beach gets crowded in the afternoon. I'm standing up doing some stretches around 2 p.m., just after Agent Colder makes her assigned radio check. I spot him casually walking down the access path coming our way. He's about 25 or 30, wearing dark sunglasses. He has on long pants, and a t-shirt, boots, and a ball cap, which is not exactly beachwear attire. However, the thing that gets my attention is that he's wearing a backpack.

I nudge Agent Colder's foot. "Check this dude out," I whisper.

We both watch as he passes us and stops about halfway to the lapping waves of the ocean. In a rather crowded area, he takes off his backpack and places it gently on the sand. He sits down beside the backpack for about 30 seconds. He then gets up and walks north along the beach towards the swash. We watch as he finally turns and cuts diagonally back toward the access path away from his backpack.

Alarms go off in my head. I don't like the looks of this. I ask Agent Colder to give Detective Concile two beeps on the police radio, which means a possible threat has appeared.

Just as I get ready to move to cut him off at the steps leading to the path, my phone rings. I look at the name of the caller and say, "Damn." I look at my phone and back at the possible threat and say, "Agent Colder, go talk to that guy and remind him he forgot his backpack, but don't reveal you're DEA. I need to take this call. I'll be right behind you."

She gives me a funny look and heads over to cut him off.

In a very professional tone of voice I say, "I'm sort of busy right now. Can I call you back later?"

The caller replies, "Looking forward to it."

CHAPTER 20

I hurry to catch up with Agent Colder. I move in just as she is confronting our possible suspect. She says, "Excuse me, but you forgot your backpack. Do you want me to keep an eye on it for you? I've seen things disappear at the beach many times."

Before he can answer, I walk up, put my arm around Agent Colder and say, "I'm sorry, my wife had her beach bag stolen once and her credit cards and other personal things were inside. She doesn't want that to happen to anyone else."

"That's not necessary," he responds. "I was just leaving it for a family to pick up later. It's full of books for their kids to read while they're at the beach."

I look at Agent Colder and say, "Great. Honey, why don't you watch the backpack for this nice gentleman while I get something from the car."

She tries to smile. "That's a good idea…dear." She turns and heads back toward our location.

I walk with my new friend. Once we get to a rather secluded area on the path, I pull my weapon, stick it in his ribs and show him my PI ID. "Turn around and put your hands on the railing." I quickly frisk him and find no weapons. "Now, I'm not going to hurt you. Just tell me who gave you the backpack."

With duress in his voice he replies, "Some guy paid me a hundred dollars to deliver it to some family members who were coming to the beach later."

I press the weapon harder into his side. "Did you look inside?"

"Yes, it's full of books."

"What did the guy look like?"

"He was tall, had an accent and a beard. Seemed like a nice enough guy."

"Did he tell you his name?"

"No. What's this all about?"

I contemplate for a few seconds then remove my weapon from his side. "Nothing. You're free to go, but if you see this man, don't mention me. I'll be watching. By the way, where did he give you the backpack?"

"I was in the Food Lion in North Myrtle Beach. As I was leaving, he asked if I could do him a favor. I declined until he said he would pay me $100."

"Did he give you specific instructions on what to do?"

"Yes, he told me where to go and to leave the backpack of books and a family would pick it up later."

"Okay, get out of here. Remember, if you see the man again, don't mention me."

Now, I have a quandary. Should I go down to the backpack? If I do, are the bad guys watching me? Is it really books or a bomb? Personally, I think the bad guys are just probing our lines to see if we are here and watching, but I don't know that for sure. The guy said he saw books. Of course, there could be explosives in the books.

Agent Colder is standing by our location as I approach. She is on her phone. "It's Detective Concile. She wants to talk to you."

She says before handing me the phone, "What's this married crap?"

I smile, ignore the comment and accept her phone. "Yes, detective."

"So what do you think? Is the backpack a possible threat?"

"I think if it was a bomb, they would have already detonated it. I think they're just probing to find out if we're here before they make their final move. See if anyone else along the beach has had a similar encounter with a backpack and tell them not to go near it, just ignore it for now."

She hesitates. "OK. I'll get right back to you."

Minutes later, she calls back. "There was another backpack just seconds ago in Windy Hill. Same scenario. We're staying away from it for now."

I reply, "Let's wait until four and see what happens."

"You know, we're playing Russian roulette with this. If either one of them is a bomb, I'm going to have to answer a lot of questions about why I didn't contact the bomb squad right away."

"Your call, detective."

After an uneasy silence, she responds. "I've got to call the bomb squad, Mickke D. I have no other choice. We can't take any chances with people's lives. Go down and get everyone away from the area of the backpack. The bomb squad will be there right away."

I offer an alternative. "Here's an idea. Why not have the lifeguards go down and secure the area. They can say they noticed the backpack and called the police, who then called the bomb squad. Maybe no one will be the wiser."

"Okay, sounds like that may be worth a try." She hangs up and within ten minutes, two lifeguards are at the site and ushering people away. Seconds later, the bomb squad shows up with several uniformed police officers. After doing some preliminary work, they carefully place the backpack in a secure container and leave the beach. We all watch the crowd to see if anyone looks out of place. We notice nothing out of the ordinary, and before long, everything is back to normal.

Fifteen minutes later, Detective Concile calls Agent Colder. "Both backpacks just had books, no explosives. They are checking for prints now. Stay alert. We are going to get more task force people walking the beach. Keep your eyes open for the black wristbands. Plan on staying until six o'clock instead of 4."

Six o'clock comes and goes with no problems. We pack up and leave the beach. Everyone is looking forward to a nice dinner and a good night's sleep before we start all over again tomorrow.

After I arrive home, I contemplate whether to return the phone call from the beach.

CHAPTER 21

At 9:00, I decide it's time to make the call. She answers on the second ring. After pausing, I ask, "Are you in town?"

"I was asked to come down and maybe help with the Homeland Security thing. I was hoping you and I could get together for a drink or dinner."

"Beverly, as I said after our meeting with GG, or whatever her name was, I don't think I'm interested in working for a covert organization like the one you work for. I really don't think I could kill someone I don't know, strictly on the word of someone else. Now, I'm not saying I haven't done some bad things in my life to some really bad people, but I was positive they were guilty and that society would be a better place without them around."

"Look, I'm not here to recruit you. I'm here to help with the threat and maybe spend some time with you."

I hesitate before saying, "As far as you and I are concerned, I think it's time to step back and re-evaluate our relationship."

From the sudden and unexplained "call ended," I see on the screen of my phone, I gather I have lost another one of my three possible sticky situations. Strike two, one more and I'm out.

Beverly is pissed. She hangs up without uttering a word. She calls GG and tells her she doesn't feel comfortable in Myrtle Beach. GG approves her return. She checks out of The Sleep Inn and goes to the airport in Wilmington where she catches the first available flight back to Atlanta. She decides it's time to do some real soul-searching on her part. Maybe it's time to change her line of work.

CHAPTER 22

Stephanie Langchester is leaving Antigua and heading to the Bahamas. She has a degree in marine biology and is a former British Intelligence agent. She and three other girls were helping Mickke D's close friend and salvage partner, retired Federal Judge Thomas Alan Cadium, aka TC, salvage an old wreck off the coast of Pawleys Island, South Carolina. The ship, The Queen Beth, was attacked and sunk back in the early 1700s.

She and the girls ended up stealing TC's yacht and most of the valuable relics they had salvaged from the sunken ship, but she wanted more. She has a copy of an old map showing where the remaining, unfound, gold, silver, and jewels, supposedly could have been buried. She selected the Bahamas so as not to be too far away from the mainland in case she decides to travel back to South Carolina to search for the buried treasure.

*****

Retired Federal Judge Thomas Alan Cadium, is still searching for the possible buried treasure. After much research and study, he has finally decided the only place it can be is Hobcaw Barony Plantation or one of the islands just across the bay from Georgetown: Rabbit Island, Hare Island, Marsh and Big Marsh Island, Middle Ground Island, or MaLady Bush Island.

He realizes the map he has is not concise enough to give an exact location, so he plans to contact the archaeology departments at Clemson University, Coastal Carolina University, and The University of South Carolina to help him. His plan is to meet with all three universities and try to put a detail together to do an archaeological dig for the possible buried treasure. This would be great for him, plus great training for the students, at all three colleges.

He will be the chief consultant on the project, and if they are not successful, at least he can then eliminate searched areas as possible locations.

CHAPTER 23

Sunday dawns with a beautiful sunrise, and we all meet again at my office and go over some basic plans for the upcoming day. Mark and Jim will be at the point today, and Agent Colder and I will be one beach access south.

On our way to the beach, we keep our eyes open for anyone following us but we spot no tails or a black SUV. Upon arriving, we set up and get ready for a full-day stakeout. We do our walks in between locations and try to look like normal tourists enjoying the beach. Agent Colder and I both spend time reading our books and I have finally succeeded in breaking her of hitting me in the arm, although there were a few times when she started but caught herself. She checks in with Detective Concile every thirty minutes and all seems to be going well.

At 11:20 a.m., that all changes. Agent Colder receives a call and I can tell by the look on her face something is wrong. Without saying a word, she hands the phone to me.

It's Detective Concile. "We weren't the target. They just hit Charleston. Two car bombs and a propane truck blew up. The city is in panic mode. Keep your eyes open. We could still be a secondary target."

She hangs up before I can say anything or ask any questions. I immediately call Mark and Jim and give them the news. I advise them to stay vigilant.

Detective Concile calls back 20 minutes later and fills us in with what she has learned about what went down in Charleston. At 10:45 a.m., a car bomb went off in the parking lot of the Visitors Center. At 10:55 a.m., a car bomb went off at the Market Center, and at 11:15 a.m., a propane truck exploded on the Ravenel Bridge as people were trying to get away from the other explosions. Several people died and hundreds were injured. So far, they have no suspects.

The word must have spread through social media, because within a few minutes, people start to leave the beach. Probably one-third of the sun worshippers on the beach are gone. People are getting together in groups and discussing what to do. Without the first sign of a bomb or any police warning, the bad guys have disrupted the tourism industry in Myrtle Beach. Some people are scared, yet others don't seem the least bit concerned.

We stay around the rest of the day at our assigned locations and follow the breaking story on our phones. Charleston is not a pretty sight. Luckily, the death toll is only four but more than 200 innocent people were injured and transported to local hospitals. The police and the State Patrol shut down all roads in and out of the area. The Coast Guard is patrolling the waters off shore, and the FBI is now on site.

When we get back to the office and after Agent Colder leaves, I ask Jim to call his contact at the Bureau to get the latest update. He gets an okay to put him on speakerphone so all three of us can listen.

They have camera footage of one male driving into the Visitors Center in the car that ultimately exploded. He drove around three times waiting for a parking space to open up close to the center. He had on a hat, a long-sleeve shirt, and jeans. He knew where the cameras were because he covers his face at the right time. Fifteen minutes after he leaves, the car explodes.

The second car caught on camera parks along the street next to the market. One male and one female exit the car and leave. Neither one of their faces can be seen. Ten minutes after the first explosion, the car at the market explodes.

The propane truck is also captured on camera traveling north on the bridge. The driver pulls over near the middle of the bridge, acts as if he is having engine problems, and puts the hood up. Another car pulls up and offers him a ride. Just as the police are approaching the scene of the stalled vehicle, it explodes in a huge ball of fire. Both sides of the bridge are still closed. No one knows if there was any structural damage to the bridge, and they probably won't know for weeks. They do have a description of the car that picked up the driver of the truck, but it was later found abandoned.

Jim thanks his contact for the update. After he hangs up, we just sit there and don't say anything for several minutes.

*****

We all spend the last day of the holiday weekend at the beach, which is not nearly as crowded as the first two days. The beach-goers are more reserved than normal. Everyone seems on edge.

The day is boring and there are no problems. We are all happy the weekend is over. Agent Colder heads to Detective Concile's office for a de-briefing and the rest of us head home. I ask Agent Colder to call me about going down to see our possible drug dealer. She tells me she will call me tomorrow.

CHAPTER 24

Agent Colder calls me early Tuesday morning and agrees to meet me at my office around ten. We do not call Condo Enterprises for an appointment. We are going to make a surprise visit and see if she recognizes Jeffrey Barrons.

As we pull into the parking area, I notice a black SUV parked in the front row. While I am writing down the license number, I say to Agent Colder, "Jim said we were followed to the beach the first morning by a black SUV. Stay alert and by the way, what name do you want to use?"

She thinks for a second. "I have a close friend back on Lake Norman named Toni Swartz. Let's use that.

"Sounds good to me. Toni Swartz it is."

"So am I allowed to ask questions?" she asks.

"Why don't you just observe until we see how it's going to go. Besides that, you're not acquainted with the case. I'm going to tell them you're a new agent with our company." I can tell she's not happy with that scenario, but she agrees. I continue, "So if you think he could be your guy, why don't you say something like, 'Nice office, Mr. Barrons."

"Okay, and then what?" she asks.

"Well, I guess it will depend on whether Bob Linde is in the room. We couldn't find anything on him. He's a ghost." I pause, "If you think Barrons is your man, I think we should cut the interview short and leave. You can decide what you want to do later. I don't think he's going anywhere, do you?"

"Probably not, but I would much rather arrest him right away."

"Okay, let's do this. If Linde is in the room, and you think Barrons is your guy, I'll take Linde and you take Barrons. If we're wrong, you can apologize later."

She frowns. "Okay. Now, one more question. What if one of them recognizes me?"

"Same deal. If Linde is in the room, I'll take him, you take Barrons."

"Okay." She checks her weapon. "Ready?"

"Let's do it," I respond, but I'm a little nervous working with a partner who I don't really know. I'm hoping she has her head screwed on straight.

We enter the office. I hand the receptionist my card and ask to see Mr. Barrons. She says he is in a meeting with Mr. Linde. I ask her to tell him I only need a few minutes to ask him some questions about Mary Kay's death.

She returns shortly and tells us Mr. Barrons will see us in the conference room. She leads us there and says he will be right in and to take a seat. We both thank her but remain standing.

Two minutes later, Jeffrey Barrons walks in and closes the door behind him.

CHAPTER 25

TC arrives at the Hobcaw Barony Visitor Center to meet with representatives from the archaeology departments of Clemson University, Coastal Carolina and the University of South Carolina. A supervisor for the Belle W. Baruch Foundation for Hobcaw Barony, a private nonprofit foundation created to conserve Hobcaw Barony's unique natural and cultural resources for research and education, is present, as well. They have gathered to discuss a potential joint venture to look for the possible buried pirate treasure.

After a little background information on himself, TC holds up the logbook he found on the Queen Beth. "Ladies and gentlemen, I found this logbook buried in the sand next to the Queen Beth, a pirate ship sunk in the early 1700's, off the coast of Pawleys Island." After several gasps and murmurs, he holds up the primitive map, incased in plastic, he found in the logbook. "And I found this hand-drawn map inside the logbook which I believe shows where the captain of the ship buried his bounty." The group is speechless. He tells them after the presentation they are welcome to come up and inspect the logbook and the map. He knows he has them in his hip pocket as he begins his presentation. Now, he just needs to close the deal.

He goes into detail about finding the logbook and he reads the pages that pertain to how and where Captain Swinely buried the treasure. He tells them he believes that since the map shows what appear to be structures on the left side of a bay, a ship, and the land where the treasure was buried on the right, with the X and the wavy lines, it has to be Winyah Bay, and the structures are on the present site of Georgetown. He believes the location of the buried treasure has to be on Rabbit Island, Hare Island, Hobcaw Barony, or MyLady Bush Island. He never mentions the fact that Captain Swinely may have come back later and dug up the treasure himself.

Several people ask if they can get copies of the logbook and the map, but TC refuses until they have a signed agreement in place. He suggests that if they find the treasure, he wants half and the other half can be split any way they may wish.

After many, many questions and many looks at the logbook and map, everyone agrees to meet at the Visitor Center again in two weeks with some sort of a game plan. TC leaves with a very good feeling that finally he will be able to begin his search for Captain Kent Swinely's buried treasure.

*****

The representatives all convene two weeks later at the Visitor Center. A spokesperson for the group begins the discussion "We do not believe Captain Swinely would have buried the treasure on any of the islands because most are at sea level and the ground may have been too marshy for burying anything. We think he would have gone to higher ground on Hobcaw Barony and probably not very far on shore because of the weight of the treasure."

TC nods his head. "That makes sense. So where do we go from here?"

The spokesperson replies, "First, we need grant money and no reputable grant company would ever give money for a treasure hunt dig based on a logbook and a crude map."

TC solves that problem by asking, "How much do you need?"

They put their heads together and come up with a ballpark number of $30,000 to begin with.

"That is no problem, but since I'm footing the bill, I would like to add to the agreement that if we recover anything, I get my initial investment back off the top and then the split is 50/50." Everyone agrees.

Next, they suggest they have students set-up a grid system and do some metal detector sweeps and ultrasound detection sweeps along the shoreline across from Georgetown to see if they can pick-up any possible locations. They plan to go no more than about 200 yards inland from the shoreline. If they detect something, the area will be marked and then the fun begins.

TC loves the plan and asks when they can begin. Everyone attending seems to think a detail could be organized in about three weeks if all the permits can be secured. They all sign the agreements and TC leaves the meeting light in his checkbook but a happy camper nevertheless.

CHAPTER 26

Agent Colder is looking out the window as Jeffrey Barrons enters the conference room and closes the door behind him. She turns as I make the introductions. "Mr. Barrons, this is Toni Swartz, a new agent with our company. She's working on Mary Kay's case."

Agent Colder walks over, shakes hands with Mr. Barrons, and says, "Nice to meet you, Mr. Barrons. You have a lovely office."

Adrenaline soars through and kick starts my body. Here we go, I'm thinking.

Before Mr. Barrons can release his handshake with Agent Colder, she has twisted his wrist behind him and slammed his face on the conference room table. Blood dribbles from his broken nose.

"You're under arrest for drug trafficking, Mr. Barrons." She reads him his rights, pulls her handcuffs, places them on him and just like that, Mr. Barrons is no longer a threat.

I am impressed. This girl is good. That was quite a show.

"What do you think you're doing, you no good, crazy bitch! You have nothing on me!" Mr. Barrons yells as he tries to stand upright.

"Nice talk, Jose." She slams his head down on the table again.

Just as I am about to intervene and keep her from a lawsuit, three shots smash through the fabricated wood conference room door. The first two miss everyone, but the third one finds its way into the leg of Jeffrey Barrons.

"Kill the bastards, Luis, kill them all!" Barrons screams as he topples to the floor of the conference room.

I look at Agent Colder and she returns my stare as we both back away from the door. I hear running in the hallway and carefully open the door with Agent Colder covering me. I quickly say, "You good here?"

"I'm good. Go!"

I move into the hallway leading to the reception area. As I enter the reception vicinity, employees are popping their heads up with terrified looks on their faces. I quickly ask, "Everyone okay?" No one answers. They just nod their heads. "Someone call 911. Where did he go?" I ask.

As I stare at their blank faces, finally the girl at the front desk answers, "He went out the front door. I already called 911."

I hustle to the front door and watch as the black SUV spins out of the parking lot and ventures toward 17 Bypass. I get on my cell phone and call Detective Concile. "I'm rather busy, Mickke D. I just had a call about a shooting at Condo Enterprises." After a slight pause, and no response from me, she continues, "Oh God, don't tell me you're involved."

"I'm afraid so. Agent Colder just arrested Jeffrey Barrons and his partner Bob Linde fired at us through the conference room door. We're fine but he hit his boss in the leg. He just left the parking lot in a black Chevy Tahoe. South Carolina license 1746-SLM."

CHAPTER 27

Marty, Ronnie, Phil, and Anna (as they are called in America), are drinking a toast at their safe house and already planning their next attack. If all goes well, it could happen within the next two weeks.

Marty and Ronnie are from Syria while Phil and Anna are from Yemen. They are not martyrs; they want to live so they can continue their attacks on the West. They were all raised to hate the West, particularly Americans.

All four speak fluent English with a slight accent; however, Anna does most of the shopping. They dress as Americans and show no trend toward terrorism. Once they arrive at their destination, they rent a house out in the country, away from the hustle and bustle of the big city. Anna rents a P.O. Box and they receive cash every week to fulfill their needs. They are funded by factions of ISIS and the Taliban.

Following their next attack, they will move on to New Orleans, then Nashville, Columbus, Ohio, Boston, and finally New York City. They will then return to Canada and back to the Middle East, leaving a path of destruction behind them.

CHAPTER 28

Bob Linde abandons the Tahoe and takes an Uber to his safe house. When he and Jeffrey Barrons arrived in town, they rented a condo under an assumed company name and purchased a second car in case of an emergency. At the condo, there are weapons and disguises to wear. He will be able to traverse the area with no problem.

He knows the Feds have Jeffrey and that they are now looking for him. He believes Jeffrey will not snitch on him, so he has two choices: He can leave town and head back to New York, or he can stay and do the job he agreed to do, get rid of Mickke D. He decides to stay, finish the job and collect the money before moving on.

*****

Agent Colder and I are waiting in the conference room when Detective Concile arrives. The EMTs are giving first aid to Jeffrey Barrons' gunshot injury, which turns out to be no more than a flesh wound. She's not a happy camper.

"So what happened here and why wasn't I informed of your plans?"

Agent Colder and I look at each other and I point to her, "Go ahead, it was your bust."

She begins, "Well, we came down here to see if I recognized Mr. Barrons as a drug dealer and I did. I arrested him and then his partner started shooting at us through the door," pointing at the bullet holes in the conference room door.

"And how did Mr. Barrons get a bloody nose?"

"She attacked me for no reason whatsoever. I'm going to sue everyone here!" Barrons exclaims.

"Oh shut up, you were resisting arrest." Agent Colder replies.

"Is that true Mickke D?" Detective Concile asks.

I look at Agent Colder. "That's how it looked to me, detective."

"They're lying! I want my attorney. They're both lying! She attacked me. I'm going to sue!" screams Barrons.

"Can you hold him until I can get someone down here from Charlotte to pick him up?" Agent Colder calmly asks.

"No problem, Agent Colder, consider it done. I'll expect both of you in my office this afternoon to provide a written account of what happened."

CHAPTER 29

Two days later, I'm nowhere close to figuring out what happened to Skipper Chucks, Linda Evans, and Mary Kay Henderson. Jeffrey Barrons lawyered up and said nothing before being transported to Charlotte by Agent Colder and another DEA agent. No one can find Bob Linde. They found the Tahoe but it had been wiped clean. He seems to have disappeared. I keep thinking that it is all related but I have no idea how.

Just as I am about to close the file folders on my desk, Jannie transfers a call to me from one of my old real estate clients. "Hey, Mickke D, it's Doug and Nancy Scottish. You found us a home out in Longs on Gator Ridge Road about a year ago. You said if we ever needed anything to be sure and call."

"Sure, Doug, I remember you two. How can I help you?"

"Well, it's funny. We had this couple move in just down the road from us about two months ago. Real quiet folks. Then two guys seemed to move in with them. They keep all the blinds closed in the house and they don't seem to work. They have an old car and a van and it looks like they turned the garage into a storage area. I remember you had a private investigation company and well, it looks real fishy to me. Could you stop by sometime and see what you think? I called the sheriff but he said unless they do something wrong, he can't do anything."

"Doug, I'd be happy to stop by and visit with you guys. I'll call before I head out your way. May not be for a day or two, but I will stop by."

"Thanks, we're looking forward to seeing you," Doug replies.

*****

The following day after lunch, I stop in Jim's office and ask, "Hey, big guy, would you like to take a ride out to Longs with me? One of my real estate clients thinks something fishy is going on in the neighborhood, so I told them I would stop by."

"Sure, should I bring my weapon?"

"I guess so, why not."

I call Doug and tell him we're on our way. Thirty minutes later, we pull into Doug's driveway on Gator Ridge Road. They both come out to greet us. I notice both sets of eyes go to Jim's weapon as Doug says, "Thanks for stopping by, Mickke D. I think these people are up to no good."

"Doug and Nancy, this is Jim Bolin. He's in charge of the PI business."

"Nice to meet you, Mr. Bolin," Doug says as they both shake hands with Jim. Doug says, "Oh, here they come now."

We all watch as an old gold Chevy Impala comes slowly down the road. Doug and Nancy wave at them. Their wave is not returned. "See, what did I tell you? When was the last time you waved at someone in South Carolina and they didn't wave back?"

I gaze at Jim before answering, "It's been a long time, Doug."

We all watch as the two occupants pull into the driveway next door, which is about fifty yards away, exit the car and look our way before getting sacks of groceries out of the trunk. They still don't wave, although I seem to notice a curt smile on the partially hidden face of the woman.

I finally say to Doug, "I'll run the tax records for that property and see if I can find out who owns it. I'll get back to you one way or another. Have you ever spoken to them?"

"No, we knocked on their door right after they moved in and they never answered the door. Nancy and I keep thinking they may be terrorists or something."

I look at Jim and reply, "Well, in this day and age, one never knows."

*****

Phil and Anna notice the four people as they pass by. They glance again as they get out of their car. "Did you notice one of those guys has a weapon? Do you think they are the police?" Anna whispers to Phil.

"I don't know, but maybe we should consider moving. We don't need the police knocking on our door."

Once inside the doublewide structure, they pull the blinds apart and watch as the two men leave their neighbors' house. Phil calls for a meeting. The discussion is hot and heavy, but in the end, all four agree on their next plan of action.

*****

As we're driving back to the office I say, "So what do you think?"

"Well, I think they have read too many murder mystery novels or they need to find something else to do all day rather than spy on their neighbors. What do you think?"

"Well, I don't know. Their neighbors did seem a little strange. I'll check the tax records and see what I can find out."

Once in the office, I get on my computer and run the tax records for the parcel of land next to Doug and Nancy. I find the owner's information. They live in Richmond, Virginia, and I give them a call. The call goes to voicemail, so I leave a message that I am a real estate broker and I may have someone interested in purchasing the property, and to please give me a call back.

CHAPTER 30

The following morning I am reading the paper and half listening to the Weather Channel, when my cell phone rings. It's Jim. "Did you hear about the fire?"

My first thought was that the office burned down. An assassin almost burned it to the ground not long ago. "Oh God, not the office."

"No, not the office. Doug and Nancy's house burned to the ground last night along with their neighbors' house. Go to the local ABC channel, they're showing it right now."

I quickly switch channels and get a sick feeling in my stomach as I see the smoldering remains of Doug and Nancy's house and their neighbor's house. The reporter says that the fire consumed both homes and two occupants of one of the homes died in the fire.

I get back on my phone. "Are you still there?"

"Yeah," Jim replies, "what do you want to do?"

I think for a few seconds. "First of all, I'm going to call Sam and try to find out what she knows. I'll get back to you."

Detective Concile answers on the first ring. "It's awfully early Mickke D, this had better be good."

"Okay, but before you say anything, hear me out."

"Whatever, go ahead, you have my full attention." she sarcastically replies.

"Did you hear about the fire last night in Longs where two people died?"

"Yes, I did. Saw it on the local news this morning."

I continue, “Well, the couple that lived in one of the houses were real estate clients of mine and they called me to come out and check on what they referred to as some fishy neighbors. Jim and I went out there yesterday afternoon, met with them and actually saw two of the neighbors, a man and a woman.”

“And your point is?” she asks.

“Let me finish. They also told us that after the man and woman moved in, two men moved in with them a few days later, and that they kept all of the blinds closed and they turned their garage into a storage area. Doug and Nancy, the couple who are clients of mine, thought they were terrorists. I ran the county records and found the owner of the property. I called and left a message, but never heard back from them.”

After what seemed like an eternity, she finally says, “You have got to be kidding me. You think they could be terrorists?”

“Not only just terrorists, but possibly the ones who blew up Charleston. Think about it. Every road was closed leaving the area and yet they were never found. Maybe they never left. Maybe they’re still here for a reason. I don’t know but if I were you, I would get someone out there to check it out.”

“I can’t send anyone, that’s county. However, I will make a call and have someone in charge out there today. I’ll let you know what happens.”

CHAPTER 31

Marty, Ronnie, Phil, and Anna started packing the car and the van as soon as it turned dark. They rented the house furnished so, except for some personal items, the only things going with them were food, weapons, bomb parts and components. Once loaded, they wiped down the inside of the house to the best of their ability. However, before they leave, they plan to send a strong message to anyone who attempts to interrupt their plans. Mess with us and suffer the consequences. They watch as the lights go out at Doug and Nancy's around 11 p.m.

Just after midnight, Marty, Ronnie and Phil quietly move toward Doug and Nancy's, leaving Anna to prepare the house for their getaway. The men quickly break in through the back door. Doug and Nancy are sleeping ducks.

Doug and Nancy hear the noise. They are sitting up in bed when the intruders enter the bedroom. Doug reaches for his gun, in the dresser beside him, but before he can open the drawer, he and Nancy are each shot. Tom douses the room with gasoline from a one-gallon container they brought with them. They light a match, drop it and leave the same way they came in, jogging back to where Anna is waiting. As soon as she sees the fire from the house next door, she lights a match and starts a fire in the rented house, as well. They get into their vehicles and slowly drive away. The entire process takes less than ten minutes. There are no other homes within a half-mile so they are long gone before anyone notices the two blazes and calls the authorities.

They spend the night in a building about three miles away, which they leased, under an assumed name, for three months when they first arrived. They told the owner they were going to start an auto painting shop and if it proved successful, they would lease the building long term. The only auto painting they have done is to paint their vehicles after the Charleston bombing and to use it as a storage area for their explosives. They spend the night painting the vehicles again.

The next day around noon, Phil and Anna move into an RV park not far from the ocean, renting a large, furnished RV for a month with cash. They tell the park manager they are thinking about moving to the beach and want to check it out before making a final decision. Marty and Ronnie arrive later. They park both newly painted vehicles on the side of the RV, partially hidden from the road. Their spot is near the back edge of the park and not many of the RV's around them are occupied. Most of the owners use the park as a winter retreat and don't rent them out to the tourists. It's closer quarters than what they would like, so they need to be extremely careful and not raise any red flags. They are planning for their attack to begin in about ten days.

CHAPTER 32

Sam calls me right after lunch. She contacted the proper authorities and gave them the info I had given her. They informed her that from what they had found, both people in the one house, a man and a woman, had been shot, and no one was found in the second home. From the retrievable evidence at the scene of the fire, the occupants were Doug and Nancy Scottish. She said they wanted to talk to Jim and me ASAP.

An hour later, we meet with Captain Norma Kirkpatty of the Horry County Police Department at their Little River office behind the library. We fill her in with everything we know and she thanks us for our input. She asks if we could give her any type of a description of the neighbors, but we were too far away to get a good look at their faces, so our descriptions were very sketchy to say the least, but I do remember that curt, faint, smile on the woman's partially scarf covered face. We did give her a description of the vehicles parked in the driveway.

Captain Kirkpatty tells us she will put out a BOLO on the two vehicles and hope someone may spot them. She will ask the public to help by keeping an eye out for two vehicles possibly used in a recent crime without telling them they may be terrorists. There is no need to panic the public yet.

As we are leaving, I look at Jim. "I think they're still close by. If they were planning something, I don't believe they would just pack up and leave. What do you think?"

"Yeah, I think you're right, but where are they and what are they planning?"

CHAPTER 33

Three days after the fire, I am waiting in line at the Post Office, located in a hardware store on Sea Mountain Highway. I finally get my stamps and before leaving, I stop at the popcorn stand and pick up a container of fresh, hot popcorn. Now, I learned a long time ago that if I try to take the popcorn with me in my SUV, I usually spill it all over the front seat; therefore, I am aimlessly wandering around the store eating popcorn when I notice a young woman enter the store. One of the employees welcomes her, and there it is, that same curt, faint smile, I remember seeing on the face of the woman who lived next door to Doug and Nancy. My popcorn ends up on the floor instead of on the front seat of my vehicle. I nonchalantly act as if nothing has happened and tell the nearest employee I will be happy to clean up the mess. The employee tells me she will take care of it. The woman looks my way but doesn't act as if she recognizes me. She just turns and continues her trip toward the Post Office section of the store.

I watch her as she goes in the direction of the Post Office boxes. I quickly leave the hardware store. On my way to my vehicle, I look around the parking lot and notice a Chevy Impala, which looks a lot like the one parked next door at Doug and Nancy's. The only problem is that it is black instead of gold. I move my vehicle to the far end of the parking lot and call Jim. "I think one of Doug and Nancy's fishy neighbors is at the Post Office."

"No way, did you confront them?"

"No, I'm out in my vehicle waiting for her to leave."

"Are you going to call Sam or Captain Kirkpatty?"

"No, not until I'm sure she's who I think she is. But, what I need you to do since I'm waiting in the parking lot is to come down here. I'll be at the far end of the lot closest to the IGA. If I'm gone, it means I'm following her. I want you to go inside and see if you can find out if she purchased anything and then call me."

"No problem, boss, I'm on my way."

*****

Anna remembered her training. She did notice the man who spilled the container of popcorn and he did look familiar. He could have been one of the guys she saw at their neighbor's house the other day. She continued toward the Post Office section of the store where she was going to pick up another cash delivery from her P.O. box and then purchase some items on her shopping list.

If it is him, she doesn't believe he will start anything in a public location and she can't afford to spoil their plans by starting a battle of her own.

Within minutes, she finds what she is looking for and carefully ventures toward the checkout counter. She does not see the bumbling idiot who spilled the popcorn or any sign of the police. She pays for her items with cash and slowly leaves the store. She has one hand in her purse, which holds her snub-nose .38, and she is prepared to use it. She casually glances in both directions before crossing to her car in the parking lot. She notices a vehicle parked at the far end towards the IGA, which looks familiar, but doesn't want to stare in case it is him and he may be watching her. She errs on the side of caution. She leaves the parking lot and proceeds toward Ocean Boulevard. She turns right and obeys the speed limit while keeping an eye in her rear-view mirror to see if he is following her.

CHAPTER 34

I watch as the woman in question exits the store and gets into the black Impala. She slowly turns left on Sea Mountain Highway and then turns right on Ocean Boulevard. I wait until she is out of sight, and then make my way toward Ocean Boulevard. I have this gut feeling she knows I am on to her. I turn right one block before Ocean Boulevard on Spring Street and keep my eyes peeled for her to show up in front of me where the two streets intersect.

I am aware that if she is a terrorist, this could be a dangerous game of cat and mouse. I need to stay on my toes. I am all of a sudden convinced she is one of the persons we saw next door to Doug and Nancy's the other day, so I call Sam.

She answers after two rings. "Now what?"

"Do you have any unmarked cars in the Ocean Boulevard area of Cherry Grove?"

"What are you up to now, Mickke D?"

"I'm looking for one of the neighbors who lived in the house next to Doug and Nancy. I spotted her in the post office a few minutes ago. They painted the vehicle. The gold Impala is now black."

"Are you sure it's her?"

"I'm positive."

Silence, then, "Okay, but don't get too close. We need all of them, not just one. Where are you?"

"I'm just passing Tillman Resort heading south."

"And where is she?" she quickly asks.

I'm not sure, she is somewhere in front of me. Hold on, Jim is calling."

I put her on hold. "Hey big guy. What did you find out?"

"Nothing good. She purchased two pounds each of nuts, bolts and nails. Are you thinking pipe bomb?"

"And how did you find that out?" I ask before wishing I had not.

"I've played golf with the guy who checked her out."

For some reason, I'm not surprised. "Thanks Jim, I've got Sam on the phone. Go back to the office and see if you can round up Mark. I'll get back to you."

I click the hold button. "Still there, detective?"

"Still here, have you spotted her yet?"

"No, but Jim just told me she purchased nuts, bolts and nails at the hardware store."

"Damn! Okay, give me a description of her and the car she's driving."

"It's a black Chevy Impala, maybe 05' or 06'. She's probably late twenties or early thirties with black hair. She's wearing blue jeans, a green blouse and a brown baseball cap."

"All right, keep looking and let me know if you see her. Do not engage. We need all of them. We need to know where they are. Is that clear?"

"I understand, detective. I'll keep you advised."

What I don't understand is how she disappeared. I speed up hoping to catch sight of her. I get to Main Street and she is still nowhere to be found. I've lost her.

*****

Anna wasn't taking any chances. She turns into the first parking garage she sees and waits for her possible tail to appear. The parking garage has an entrance off Ocean Boulevard and an exit on to Spring Street, one block back from Ocean Boulevard. Within minutes, the fumble bum from the hardware store passes the garage on Spring Street. She was right. He looks like one of the guys who was at her neighbor's house the other day, and he's in the same vehicle she spotted in the parking lot of the hardware store.

She leaves the garage and goes back to Sea Mountain Highway. While keeping her eyes on the rear-view mirror, she goes west to 17 before turning south and going back to the RV park. She passes the entrance of the park twice before actually turning in, just to be safe.

When Anna arrives at the RV, another meeting takes place. She gives a full debrief as to what took place and how easily she lost her pursuer. The group decides to stay on track and for Anna not to venture outside for a while. One of the others will run any errands, that need done. They also decide to have Anna bleach her hair and to get rid of the green blouse and brown ball cap. Tonight after it gets dark, they will take the Impala back to the building and paint it again.

They need more nuts, bolts, and nails, but they don't want to buy large amounts at any one store so as not to bring attention to themselves.

They also discuss the need for another P.O. box. They figure the police will be waiting for Anna if she goes back to the box at the hardware store. They make a call and tell their money benefactors not to send anything else to that P.O. box.

By noon the following day, they have a new P.O. box, the Impala is now silver and Anna is a blonde. They continue with their original plan and schedule. Seven days left.

CHAPTER 35

I call Sam and give her the bad news. She is not a happy camper but thanks me anyway. I return to the office and give Jim and Mark the unpleasant news as well.

"Well, at least we know they're still here," Mark says, "I guess that's a plus."

"Right, but I still can't believe I lost her and we still don't know where they are. Jim, see if you can find out where they could have gotten their vehicles painted that quickly. I suppose you've played golf with some owners of body shops as well."

"Don't think so, but I'll see what I can find out," he replies with a big grin on his face. "By the way, I asked the guy at the hardware store if he had ever seen the woman in the store before and he said not that he could remember."

I quickly reply, "That's strange, because I watched her go over to the P.O. boxes at the post office."

Mark says, "Maybe she just got the P.O. box."

"Without a name, there's no way to check that out. I didn't see which box she went to. Okay Jim, how many people from the post office have you played golf with? See if you can find out anything about the P.O. box as well. Thanks guys, we need to stay on top of this."

After Jim and Mark leave my office, I put my feet up on my desk and wonder if I'm getting too old for this type of work. How did I lose that woman that quickly?

I jump in my SUV and go back down to the scene of my embarrassing failure. I take the route she took and not the route I took. As soon as I see the parking garage on my right, I figure it out. She popped in here and as soon as I went by, she backtracked and left the area. How could I be so stupid as to have not looked into the parking garage? However, if I had, she may have run or started shooting and we would never have figured out where the rest of them are staying. That's my story and I'm sticking to it. Not sure about the logic, but it definitely makes me feel better.

An hour later, Jim returns to my office. "Well, I got the down and dirty on the P.O. box. A woman rented a box three days ago for one month, which would have been the timeframe we're looking at. Of course, they would not give me any names or addresses but they did say she paid in cash."

"Well, we all know the name and address doesn't exist. And should I ask how in the world you got that information?" I ask.

"Well, I took my golfing buddy from the checkout counter back to the post office to vouch for me, showed them my PI license and said it was a matter of national security."

"You never cease to amaze me," I comment.

He continues, "And they are going to put a hold on everything going to that P.O. box."

"Great, but when Sam calls to find out why we're messing around with her investigation, I'm going to have her contact you."

"No problem, I'll claim client/PI confidentiality."

I change the subject. "So anything on the body shops yet?"

"No, but that's next on my list."

"Stay on your toes. If they figure out I was tailing her and who we are, they may come after us, as well."

CHAPTER 36

Bob Linde is getting antsy. He's been laying low for over a week and he thinks it's about time to make his move. He knows where Mickke D's office is and he found his home address online. His only decision now is which one of these places would be the easiest to attack. He had no problem with the couple who saw Jeffrey and him at the marina, or Mary Kay at her apartment, but this one may not be quite as easy.

He decides he will have a better chance of getting out of town after dark. He packs up some personal things and has everything in his vehicle when he arrives at Mickke D's home address around 10 p.m.

*****

I'm watching TV and Blue is curled up on the couch sound asleep. I hear a car go by slowly. The police patrol the area so my apprehension goes away quickly but not for long.

Blue's head comes up from the couch and a low growl resonates from deep in his belly. I do not hesitate, I whisper for Blue to "stay," grab my .45 from the table next to my chair, and quietly open the sliding glass door to my porch. I am out with little or no sound. I go around the deck and down the stairs to the side of the house where I gingerly continue to the corner of the garage. I peer around the corner and see a strange car parked across the street from my driveway. There are no lights on, but the motor is running.

I invited no one to come over and no one called to say they were coming over so I'm guessing this is not a friendly visit. My only problem is how many came to visit. As I come around in front of the garage door, I hear a trigger being cocked and I stop. Next, I hear my doorbell ring and Blue barks.

The time has come to engage. I take a step around the corner of the house and ask, "Are you looking for me?" while pointing my gun at the lone figure's back. I see what looks like a sawed-off shotgun hanging from his right arm. "Drop the scatter gun, raise your hands and turn around slowly or I'll blow your head off."

My uninvited guest says without turning or dropping the weapon, "Sorry, I must have the wrong address."

His accent and voice are a dead give-away. It's Bob Linde. "Mr. Linde, I am only going to say this one more time. Un-cock your weapon and let it drop to the ground."

I hear the click and the gun falls to the concrete stoop. As he starts to raise his right hand, I notice his left hand goes around toward his stomach. Before he can pull a weapon and make the turn, I fire one time. Linde falls to his knees and keels over on my front stoop. A pistol drops from his left hand.

I walk up, kick both weapons away, and feel his neck for a pulse. There is a weak pulse so I immediately go inside, call 911 and ask them to send an emergency vehicle to my address.

My next call is to Detective Sam's cell phone. She answers after three rings. "Do you have any idea what time it is?"

"Yes, I do. Bob Linde just tried to kill me. You had better come over to my house. I already called 911."

"You okay?" she asks.

"Yeah, I'm fine."

"Is Linde dead?"

"No, I think he is still alive but just barely."

"I'll call it in and be right there."

I end the call, walk back outside and just as I reach my yard, Jim comes charging out of his house and runs toward me with gun in hand. I hold up my hand and yell out, "It's me, Jim, stand down. It's over."

He slows to a walk and lowers his weapon. "What the hell happened? I was in the bathroom when I heard the gunshot."

"Yeah, and so did all my neighbors." I watch as porch lights and garage lights go on across the street at Mary Ann's and my next-door neighbor Elaine's, as well as most of the homes on the cul-de-sac.

Within minutes, the EMTs come down the street, followed by a police cruiser and stop in front of my house. Now, I look around and it seems as if the entire street is filled with neighbors looking my way. Detective Sam pulls up seconds later. "Mickke D, I'm surprised your neighbors don't ask you to move. You're bad news for the local real estate market."

"Very funny, detective." I murmur.

She looks at the EMTs as they come by with Bob Linde on a gurney and asks, "Is he going to make it?"

One of them with "Tim" on his uniform answers, "Well, he's alive now. We'll get him to the hospital as quickly as we can."

I look at Sam and say, "You need to see if you can find out why he came after me."

"That's my job, Mickke D. I'll see what I can find out." She turns to face Jim and says, "Mr. Bolin, have you been questioning employees at the post office in Cherry Grove claiming to be with Homeland Security?"

Jim gets that Who me? look on his face, "No way, detective. I have never claimed to be with Homeland Security. I may have asked them a few questions but that was all."

"Okay, both of you. Tomorrow morning, 10 o'clock, my office, be there." She turns and walks away.

Jim half-whispers, "We seem to spend a lot of time at her office. Do you think she's pissed or just messing with us. Damn, I have an 8:30 tee time in the morning."

"Probably a little bit of both. I guess you'll have to call first thing in the morning and cancel your tee time. I'll pick you up about 9:40."

Once everyone finally leaves, I get a bucket of water and a brush to clean the blood off my stoop. Just as I begin, Mary Ann, my very attractive single neighbor from across the street, who just recently moved in, walks over and says, "I know I haven't lived here long, but does this happen often at your house? I was just talking to Bill and Hazel, and they said it's happened before."

"Oh, no, Mary Ann, just a couple of misunderstandings. Hopefully, this will be the last one."

"That's good, because I moved down here to the beach for some peace and quiet. This is not peace and quiet." She turns and walks back across the street to her house before I can reply. Sounds like I probably won't be on her Christmas card list.

CHAPTER 37

We arrive at Sam's office about 9:55 and we are ushered into her office. She begins by saying, "Mr. Linde made it through surgery, but he's still in recovery. I'll let you know if I find out anything. I also notified Agent Colder at DEA to come pick him up. He can share a cell with Jeffrey Barrons. So, Mickke D, tell me what happened last night."

I give a detailed explanation of how the whole incident came about and then she asked me to write it all down and sign it. She could have just said to write it down in the beginning, but I think she wanted to make it as time-consuming as possible.

Next, she jumps on Jim for talking with the employees at the post office without consulting her first and then tells him and me to write down exactly what took place at the hardware store. She also reminds me that I lost the suspect and maybe the possibility of finding the entire crew of terrorists. I was very much aware of that without her bringing it up again.

Finally, she tells us to keep our eyes open but that the police will handle the situation from this point forward. I interject by saying, "But I'm the only one who has seen her. Don't you want me to keep looking for her?"

Without changing expression she replies, "What you do during your normal daily investigations is up to you. I'm just telling you this is a police matter. And I just know you will keep me advised if you discover anything."

"Absolutely, detective. You'll be the first person I call. And I know that if anything comes up on your end with Bob

Linde or you find out something that may help us with our daily investigations, you will let us know as well."

"Don't push your luck, Mickke D. Now both of you get out of here."

*****

Two days later, Jim comes into my office and tells me he could not find any body shops in the area that might have painted the Impala, but one shop manager told him about a possible body shop out in the country near Longs.

A friend of the shop manager told him that he had leased his building to some people who said they were going to start an auto painting shop. The shop manager gave Jim the man's phone number. Jim called, spoke with the man, and got the address in Longs. The man described the couple who leased the building and it sounded like the couple next door to Doug and Nancy Scottish. "So, do you want to call Detective Concile, or should we go check it out?"

"What do you think? Is Mark around?"

"Yeah, I think he's in his office."

"Well, grab him. Tell him to lock and load, we're going on a recon mission."

Forty-five minutes later, we have the building in sight. It sits about seventy-five yards off the road. It looks to be about 100' x 100' with a pull-up garage door and a single solid front door. It is built with red aluminum siding and a metal roof. It seems deserted. We see no vehicles and no activity. I drive past the building, turn around and come back. We still see absolutely nothing except a building sitting in an open field with no signs or advertising.

I drive my SUV down the short road to the building and stop about fifty feet away. We still don't see any activity. I look at Jim and Mark, pull my .45, and say, "Okay guys, time to see if anyone is home and be careful, the place could be booby-trapped. Mark, you go around to the right, Jim to the left, and I'll check out the front door. Call out if you see anything and again, be careful."

The front door is solid with no window, so I can't see inside. I carefully try the doorknob and it is locked. After looking the door over, I get out a credit card and deftly slide the card into the opening and "click," the door is unlocked. I carefully turn the knob and back off as I slowly push the door inward. I slide quickly through the opening with gun in hand. After my eyes get a chance to adjust to the dark building, I see what looks like a paint-booth, compressors and cans of paint sitting around. Then I see something that makes my spine tingle. As I locate the light switch and turn the overhead lights on, I call out to Mark and Jim, "It's clear. Come on in through the front door. You need to see this."

CHAPTER 38

Marty, Ronnie, Phil, and Anna have been busy assembling their explosive devices. They brought the explosive materials with them from Canada after killing two border patrol agents at a remote crossing and evading the authorities. The three men go out daily and purchase small quantities of nuts, bolts and nails from different stores all over the beach so as not to raise any eyebrows.

Anna has pretty much been isolated in the RV, and she is beginning to get cabin fever. You can only work on explosives so long and then you get complacent. That's when accidents happen. As a blonde and with different clothes, she feels she should at least be able to go to the beach for a walk.

She leaves the RV with her purse and sub-nose .38 around 1:00 in the afternoon, and begins her walk to the beach. The three men all arrive back at the RV around 1:30 and not only is Anna not there, but she forgot to lock the front door to the RV and set the alarm. The men are livid. Phil figures she went to the beach and heads in that direction while Marty and Ronnie look around the RV. They decide no one was in the RV while everyone was gone. They then choose to take the completed devices out to the staging building in Longs. Five days left.

CHAPTER 39

"Holy shit," comes from Jim and "Oh, my God," comes out of Mark's mouth as they gaze at the ambulance unit sitting in the middle of the building. I had opened the rear doors to expose the explosives that filled up almost one-third of the rear compartment.

I carefully close the rear doors. "Don't touch anything and let's get out of here while we still can." I don't have to say it twice. They turn and quickly leave the building. I turn off the lights, and follow, pushing the button on the inside of the front door and locking the door behind me. We get back in the SUV and leave the area. About a mile away, I stop in the parking lot of a convenience store and call Sam.

"Detective, I hope you are sitting down."

"Mickke D, I have things to do. What do you want? Did you find our terrorists?" she snaps.

"No, I didn't, but I found an ambulance partially filled with explosives which I figure belong to the terrorists."

Silence on her end of the phone, and then, "Where are you?"

"Mark, Jim, and I are in Longs on Swamp Hollow Road, and we just left a building which I figure they are using to paint their vehicles and probably using as a staging area for their bombs. They have a big one there already. And I mean a really big one."

"Are you at the location now?"

"No, we're about a mile away but on the same road."

"Okay, I'm going to contact Homeland Security, the Sheriff, and I'll send a SWAT team and bomb squad out immediately."

"You may want to re-think that," I say.

"And what do you mean by that?"

"Well, from what I've seen, they have to come back at some point to pick everything up. Why not wait and catch them when they return? If you go in now, they will pack up and look for another place to operate."

"What if a bomb goes off in the meantime?"

"Detective, the only thing that would happen is that the building would be gone and there would be a big-ass hole in the ground. There's nothing within a half-mile of that building."

"Is there anywhere close by to setup a surveillance team to watch for them?"

After a short hesitation, I reply, "Yes, across the road from the building is a small wooded area which could be used for that."

As I am explaining to her where we are, I hear a vehicle coming, look up and observe a van driving by with two men in it. I stop and slowly say, "Scratch that last idea. I think the bad guys just drove by and they are headed for the building." The van looks a lot like the one parked at the house next to Doug and Nancy's house, although it is a different color.

"I'll get SWAT out there right away."

"And how long will that take?"

"Probably 30 minutes."

"That may be too long. They could be in and out by then. What do you want us to do?" I ask.

After a short pause, she replies, "I'm going to hate myself for saying this, but stop them."

"No problem, but be sure and tell SWAT we will probably be there when they arrive, and that we're the good guys."

"I'll do that," and after a slight pause, "Good luck, Mickke D. I owe you one."

CHAPTER 40

Just as Phil reaches the beach, he spots Anna coming in his direction. He finds an isolated area and waits for her. In their native language, he berates her and tells her to get her ass back to the RV.

She touches the gun in her purse but decides not to push the point right now. She apologizes for leaving the door open and not setting the alarm. She then berates him in English for speaking in their native language. They both look around to see if anyone may have heard them. No one seemed to notice.

They return to the RV in silence. They find a note that Marty and Ronnie have gone to the building in Longs to deliver some more explosives. They begin working on more bombs. The silence is deafening between them as they work. After about fifteen minutes, Anna decides the best way to resolve the problem is to lock the front door and lead Phil back to the bedroom. Thirty minutes later, they are back at work and talking to one another.

Anna is beginning to have second thoughts about this whole thing. She mentioned in several meetings that she thinks they should move on. There are too many people looking for them. The men disagree. They think they are smarter than anyone who may be trying to find them. After all, they purchased an ambulance online with cash and no one thought a thing about it. They believe the Americans are stupid, and have no idea where they are and what they are doing.

CHAPTER 41

"**So do** you think that was them?" Jim asks.

I look his way and quickly reply, "Yeah, and Detective Concile wants us to stop them. She is calling Homeland Security, the Sheriff, Horry County Police and sending a SWAT team out here, but it may be thirty minutes before they arrive."

Mark asks, "So what's the plan, boss?"

"Not sure, Mark. I hope that we'll have one by the time we get there. I'm open to suggestions."

We leave the parking area and begin our trip back to the building in silence. About halfway there, I ask, "Well, does anyone have any bright ideas?"

Jim speaks up, "Sure, let's walk in the front door and shoot their sorry asses."

"I thought about that and then I thought about that ambulance full of explosives and decided that probably would not be a good idea."

Jim replies, "You may have a point there."

"Mark, what about you? Any ideas?"

"I think we should wait until they come outside and then shoot their sorry asses."

"I like your plan better. The problem is the area is so open, it will be difficult to get close without being seen."

As we approach the building, we do not see the van. The whole area around the building is deserted. I do notice the overhead garage door is not fully closed. "Hey, do you guys remember the garage door not being completely closed?"

Mark replies, "You're right, it was all the way down when we left."

"I guess that means they have pulled the van inside and are either loading explosives or unloading explosives. Either one is not good."

We drive on by the building, turn around, and pull over so we can watch the building while deciding our next move. The only problem is that if they come out, we will be in plain sight and who knows what will happen then. We need to find somewhere to setup and be ready to attack.

I say, "Damn, I wish we had some rifles. We are going to have to be real close to do any damage with these handguns."

Mark replies, "Yea, I was thinking the same thing."

I spot the remains of an old path going into the small wooded area across the road from the building and start the vehicle. "I'm going to pull into that wooded area across the road and hopefully conceal this vehicle a little bit. We can take up positions in the trees and attack when they leave."

Mark immediately replies, "And what if they're picking up explosives and the van is full of explosives?"

"I don't think so. I think the ambulance is their main source for the explosives. They want a really big bang somewhere. Remember Charleston?"

*****

As soon as Marty and Ronnie arrive at the building, they open the overhead garage door, pull the van inside and close the door, almost. They begin removing their explosive devices. The only things left in the van are two AK-47s and several handguns. Some of the devices are placed in the ambulance and others are stacked under tables covered by sheets. Ronnie nervously asks, "Did you hear something outside?"

"Just a car going by. Trust me, our American friends know nothing about our plans. Let's get this stuff unloaded and get back to the beach. I need to have a heart-to- heart talk with Anna. And, don't let me forget, I want to arm this baby before we leave. That way I can set it off from anywhere." Marty replies.

*****

After hiding the SUV as well as we can, we take up prone positions on the ground beside the biggest trees we can find. The closer to the ground, the smaller a target we become. The trees are not very big and we all feel somewhat naked and exposed. "Okay guys, here's the plan. When they come out, wait until they turn onto the road and they are broadside to us. Mark and I will fire at the tires and Jim, fire that cannon of yours at the driver's door."

Mark whispers, "Maybe they won't come out until SWAT gets here."

I change the subject. "How is everyone fixed for ammo?"

Mark answers, "I only have what's in my gun and one more clip."

"Me too." Jim says while pulling out his .44 Super Blackhawk.

"Well you guys are better off than me. I only have what's in my weapon. I guess I wasn't planning on going to war."

Mark chuckles, "Wait until Colonel Townsend hears about this. Mickke D is not prepared for battle."

"Very funny. Okay, so everyone turn off your phones. We need this to be a surprise. And, whatever you do, don't move. They will be looking directly at us when they reach the road."

Waiting is sometimes the hardest part of war. You have too much time to think about all of the things that can go wrong. Thank goodness, today was not one of those days. Within minutes, we first hear and then notice the overhead door begin to move up. The van slowly exits the building and then stops as the man in the passenger seat opens his door, gets out and pulls down the overhead door. He then closes the padlock on the door and returns to the van. They slowly venture up the gravel drive toward the main road and stop before entering.

Marty, the driver, looks at Ronnie and points, "Is that a vehicle over there in the trees?"

Ronnie yells, "Go!" as he reaches for an AK-47 from behind his seat."

Marty slams the accelerator to the floor, but since he is on a slight incline and the driveway is gravel, he doesn't do much more than burn rubber off the tires and throws gravel everywhere. He finally lets off the gas a little bit and fishtails onto the blacktop road. Ronnie sticks the AK-47 out the driver's window in front of Marty and empties his clip. Spent cartridge shells ricochet around the two men in the van.

Before we can return fire, we are hugging the ground as bullets whiz past our bodies, knocking down limbs, and thumping into trees. "Now!" I yell, and we empty our weapons on the vehicle.

The gunfire subsides and after not going very far, the van slows and turns into a shallow ditch along the side of the road. The left side tires are flat and there are three bullet holes in the driver's door. The van's left side windows and the windshield are shattered. The van moves slowly out of the ditch and makes a half circle and retreats back toward the building. About halfway there, it comes to a complete halt.

Things grow very quiet. The next sounds we hear are the womp, womp, womp of helicopter blades coming over the horizon. At about the same time we hear sirens coming from the other direction, which belong to the Horry County Police and the Sheriff's Department. As the SWAT copter approaches, Ronnie opens the passenger door and steps out with rifle in hand. One of the SWAT team members sprays the van with a .30-caliber machine gun and hits Ronnie multiple times. He falls back against the van and slides down to the ground. He is no longer a threat.

The copter circles the van and lands on the highway a safe distance from the van and the building. Four SWAT team members emerge from the copter and take a defensive position using the copter as a shield. The police and Sheriff's Department take up a similar position blocking the highway in the other direction. We stand up and everyone with a weapon is suddenly pointing them at us. "Whoa, hold on, we're the good guys." I quickly yell out as we all raise our hands high in the air.

"Stand down. They're on our side." a SWAT member using a bullhorn, yells as all the weapons are turned back to the van. He calls out, "Come out of the van with your hands in the air."

Marty, was hit by the first round fired by Jim, and then by the machine gun. He just smiles, reaches in his shirt pocket and pushes the button on the detonator.

The blast from the explosion produces a huge ball of red and orange flames as the building is torn apart. Everyone is knocked down by the power and force of the explosion. The van, which is closest to the building, is thrown back towards the road and erupts in fire. Shrapnel flies everywhere. Several police officers are hit. None are seriously wounded. The copter shakes but stays in one piece. Several smaller explosions occur within seconds and then finally the air becomes still and quiet. Thank goodness, the explosion occurred inside a concrete block building or the results could have been much worse.

We feel the hot blast of heat from the explosion and end up about five feet backward from where we were standing. I quickly assess my body and it seems to be in one piece. "Are you guys okay?"

Mark answers first, "I think so, but my ears are ringing."

Jim says, "Okay here, but I think my eyebrows are gone."

As we slowly venture out of the woods, we see nails and bolts sticking in trees. We go down to where the van is smoldering, and the SWAT team and the police are assessing the crime scene. Both of the terrorists are dead. The head honcho from SWAT says, "Sorry we didn't get here sooner.

Are you guys okay? Detective Concile said you might be here. Looks like you slowed them down before they could get away. Thanks."

Before I can say anything, he turns away and goes about his business. I look at Jim and Mark, shake my head, and say, "Looks like we're not needed. Let's head back to the beach. These guys seem to have the situation under control. I just hope they find the other two as well."

We get back to my SUV and decide that even though we went unscathed, the SRX did not. There are two bullet holes in the side of the vehicle. "Damn, I wonder if Sam will pay to have this repaired."

Jim replies, "Don't hold your breath. I think you should just call your insurance company."

Halfway back to the beach my cell rings. It's Sam. "I need you guys to come to the station and give me a written statement of what happened, so I can cover my ass in case I get in trouble for giving you the okay to go after the bad guys."

I look sideways at Jim and in the rearview mirror at Mark and reply, "You're welcome detective. Yes, we did just get shot at and almost blown up trying to stop a couple of terrorists who wanted to blow up half of the Grand Strand, and I've got two bullet holes in my SUV to show for it. Is the city of NMB going to pay for that?"

"Come on Mickke D, you don't work for the city. Your insurance will fix it and I'll be happy to write a letter to them if you wish. And, by the way, I already told you I owed you one." After a slight hesitation and no reply from us, she adds, "If it makes you feel better, we all thank you for your help."

"We'll be there in about thirty minutes." I hang up the phone without any further comments.

Jim laughs, "You know what? I think she likes us but just doesn't want to admit it."

"Right," I say as Mark and I join in the laughter.

CHAPTER 42

Phil and Anna glance at their watches and wonder why Marty and Ronnie have not returned. It's been almost three hours since they left and they should have arrived by now. Concern shows on both of their faces although neither has mentioned the possibility of a problem.

"I'm going to call," Phil finally says.

Anna responds, "You know we're not supposed to call unless it's an emergency."

"I know, but they should have been back here an hour ago. I would consider that an emergency!" he exclaims.

"Maybe they had a problem with the van. They will call if they run into any kind of trouble," she says, trying to calm him.

He ignores her and makes the call. The phone continues to ring but no one answers. Looking at Anna, he says, "Turn on the TV to a local station."

Anna just looks his way with a blank stare and does not respond. "Now!" he yells.

She quickly takes the remote and turns on the TV.

Five minutes later, BREAKING NEWS is plastered across the screen. A woman's voice says, "Two men were killed when a building in Longs exploded about two hours ago. Stay tuned for more details. We now return you to your regularly scheduled programming."

Phil and Anna gaze at each other for several seconds but say nothing. Finally, Anna says, "All of that work for nothing."

"All of that work, what about Marty and Ronnie? They're dead."

Anna nonchalantly replies, "Hey Phil, we all knew the possible consequences when we got into this."

Phil is livid. "You know what, Anna. You're perfect for this work. You're nothing but a conniving bitch with no heart. Let's get packed up and get out of here."

"Let's not do anything rash. Let's wait and watch the news to see what they say. For all we know, it could have been an accident. Then we can make a decision. If Marty and Ronnie are dead, there's no way they could have given up our location. If they had, the police would already be knocking on our door. We're safe for now," she says in a pleading voice.

Slightly calmer, he replies, "You're right. We should think this through. That's what Marty and Ronnie would have said."

CHAPTER 43

We arrive at the police station and as soon as we enter, we hear applause. Woolever and Stratton call out, "Nice job, guys."

I whisper to Jim and Mark, "At least someone here appreciates us."

As soon as we enter Sam's office, she hands each of us a legal pad and asks us to write everything down that happened at the building in Longs. "And by the way," she says, "what were you doing out there in the first place. You were supposed to keep me advised on any new developments in the case."

"We had no concrete evidence, simply hearsay, so we went there to check it out. That's when we found the ambulance filled with explosives and I called you right away."

"Whatever, just write it down."

I ask if the authorities found any evidence at the crime scene in Longs. She tells us that since the van caught fire, there was not a lot left of the two bodies to figure out much, and, of course, everything they did find was fake. The building was totally destroyed, so there was not much evidence to find there, either. The authorities have no new clues to deal with in trying to find a connection to the two remaining terrorists.

I finish my brief written statement and look over at Jim, who is still writing. "Damn, Jim, are you writing a book?"

"No, just wanted to be precise and accurate. That's what we were taught at the Bureau."

Sam jumps in. "Leave him alone. He will probably include a lot that you forgot to include."

"So detective, anything on the other two?" I ask.

"No, I figure they are going to run. What do you think?"

"You mean you actually would like my opinion?"

Without hesitation, she replies, "Of course. You guys are the only ones who have seen them."

"I told you she likes us." Jim whispers as he winks at me. "Say detective, do you think we could do these interviews online?"

Sam sneaks a rude look at Jim but says nothing.

"I think they will eventually run but not right away. We need to find a way to draw them out," I add.

"And how do we do that?" she quickly utters.

"Here's an idea. We need to piss them off, make them mad, and make them want to seek revenge."

"And again, how do we do that?" she asks.

"You need to put out a statement that you interviewed me and I told you exactly what happened at the building in Longs. If any newspapers or TV stations would like an interview, tell them I'm available."

Sam looks at me and says, "You know, you're making yourself a target, right?"

Jim looks at me and says, "Are you nuts?"

"Jim, if we don't catch them now, they will go underground and resurface later only to kill scores of people. We need to strike now. If they come after me, hopefully, we can catch them before they get to me. I'm going to need coverage at my house around the clock and Jim and Mark can keep an eye on me during office hours."

"Okay, let's set up a security schedule. I'll contact the press," Sam says. "I know a reporter at Channel 4 who would love an exclusive interview. Let me call her right now." She makes the call and puts her phone on speaker. "I need to speak to Monnie Whitson, this is Detective Concile with the North Myrtle Beach Police."

A minute or so later, as Sam paces from one edge of the room to the other, her call is answered. "This is Monnie, how can I help you?"

Monnie, this is Detective Concile. How are you today?"

"Great, Sam, what can I do for you?"

"How would you like an exclusive interview with one of the guys who was at the building in Longs when it was blown up today?"

"Count me in. Where and when?" she quickly replies.

"How about now at the North Myrtle Beach Police Headquarters. We can do it outside in front of the building."

"I'll be there in twenty minutes."

Sam looks at me again and I nod my head. "We'll see you in twenty."

Twenty-three minutes later, Monnie walks into Sam's office with a cameraman. Sam does the introductions. Monnie is a very attractive woman with long dark hair and a nice body, probably in her mid-thirties. She introduces her cameraman as Vic.

Monnie says, "Guys, I don't mean to rush you but if we plan to get this on the evening news, we need to hurry up."

Sam gives her a thumbs up and leads everyone outside. Monnie begins her interview. "Mr. MacCandlish, I understand you're a private investigator and you were there when the building blew up in Longs this afternoon?"

"Yes, I was Monnie. "

She smiles and continues, "So what happened?"

"I saw two cowards, who, instead of fighting, just blew up a building, which caused nothing more than a big hole in the ground, and then tried to run. They were a disgrace to their friends, their cause, and their religion."

"And do you think they were the ones who set off the bombs in Charleston a few weeks ago?"

I glance at Sam and she nods her head. "I would say that's a real good possibility."

"Mr. MacCandlish, what is the name of your company and why were you out there in the first place?"

"The company is Grand Strand Investigations, and we were working another case and happened to come across the building. We called Detective Concile, who sent the Horry County Police, the Sheriff and SWAT."

Monnie ends the interview with, "There you have it, folks, an exclusive interview with an eyewitness who was at the scene of the explosion in Longs earlier this afternoon. This is Monnie Whitson with Channel 4 News, reporting from the North Myrtle Beach Police Headquarters."

*****

Phil and Anna watch the evening news and catch the interview with Mickke D. They are both appalled at his comments. Phil looks at Anna and says, "Find out where his office is and we'll show him who is a coward and who is not. He'll regret the day he ever said those things about Marty and Ronnie."

CHAPTER 44

The first two days after the interview are uneventful. Sam has an undercover car parked in my neighbor's driveway at night and one in the cul-de-sac just up the street. Another couple of officers are in a golf cart across the fairway from me with night vision glasses to keep an eye on the back of my house.

Jim and Mark keep an eye out at the office. They take turns going out the back door every thirty minutes and wander around outside looking for any signs of the two terrorists.

The third day around 10:30, Jannie calls me and says someone just delivered a package for me and asks if I want her to bring it back to my office.

The clock in my head is ticking. "Jannie, listen to me very carefully. Do not touch that package. Get up from your desk and walk out the front door right now. Do it!"

I immediately call Jim and Mark and ask them if they ordered anything and they both said no. "Okay, get out of the building right now. Go out the back door and I'll meet you there. I sent Jannie out the front door. Mark, get her and get away from the building as fast as possible."

Before leaving, I carefully move the package from Jannie's desktop and place it under her desk. On my way out the door, I call Sam and tell her what has happened and that we are leaving the building as a precaution. She said she would call the bomb squad and get them over there right away.

I catch up with everyone and we begin walking quickly away from the building down Sea Mountain Highway toward the beach. I figure it has been about five minutes since Jannie's initial call to me.

We feel the hot blast wave before we hear the explosion. After checking on everyone and finding that no one is seriously hurt, I call Sam and tell her it's too late for the bomb squad, just send the fire department. However, since the fire department is right across the street, they are already on their way.

I take it for granted our two friends either heard my interview with Monnie or read about it in the paper.

*****

Anna delivered the pipe bomb to Mickke D's office. Once she was back in her vehicle, she set the timer with her phone for six minutes, which is the time she figured it would take the girl at the desk to deliver the package to Mickke D. She was off by about one minute.

CHAPTER 45

As we slowly walk back to what is left of the office, I ask Jannie, who is visibly shaken, what did the person who delivered the package look like.

"It was a woman in a brown jacket, brown pants, and a brown ballcap.

"Did she have dark hair?" I ask.

"Not sure, it was stuffed up under her hat."

"What type of a vehicle was she driving?"

"I didn't pay any attention. Mark, will you take me home? I don't feel well."

I quickly say, "Yes, Mark, take her home and stay there with her."

Just as Mark and Jannie are leaving, Detective Concile arrives along with Woolever and Stratton. "Is everyone okay?" she asks hurriedly.

"Everybody is fine, just a little shook up," I answer.

She looks around and remarks, "Your insurance company is not going to be happy with you. This is the second time, right?"

"Yeah, I'll bet my rates are going to go up a little bit."

She mumbles, "I guess they read the paper or heard your interview."

"Yeah, I guess they did," I say, as we walk toward what used to be my front door. As we walk into the building, it looks like the brunt of the damage is to the reception area. I guess me putting the package under Jannie's desk may have helped to subdue the explosion somewhat. We walk back to my office and it seems intact, except for a lot of dust. I check the other offices and they all seem fine, although they too are quite dusty. It could have been a lot worse. At least no one was hurt and the explosion did not start a fire.

We walk back outside and I hear someone calling my name. I turn around to see Monnie Whitson with her cameraman being subdued by a police officer on the other side of the yellow plastic tape, which surrounds the crime scene. I look at Sam and she waves at the officer to allow them through.

Monnie looks at Sam and me and says, "Can we do a quick interview?"

I look at Sam and she nods her head. Monnie begins, "So we are here at yet another explosion. This one is at the office of Mickke MacCandlish, on Sea Mountain Highway in Cherry Grove. Mr. MacCandlish is the witness I interviewed a couple of days ago about the explosion in Longs. Mr. MacCandlish, do you think the two explosions are connected? Does this mean there are more terrorists on the loose?"

I look at Sam and she just shrugs her shoulders. I reply, "I think that's a real good possibility, but I'm not sure. I'll let Detective Concile answer that one."

I thank Monnie and walk away. She quickly turns to Sam and begins questioning her.

*****

Phil is livid with Anna. "What's wrong with you? Don't you know how to set a timer on a pipe bomb?"

"Yeah, I know how to set it. Screw you. Next time you deliver the bomb. Let's see if you can do any better."

Phil paces around the rented RV as Anna pulls her purse with the .38 in it closer to her. She is seriously considering making this a one-person show if Phil continues to belittle her.

Finally, Phil sits down across from her and says, "So, where do we go from here?"

She eases the pressure off of her purse, thinks about his question, and replies, "I think we should cause as much havoc as we possibly can with what explosives we have left and then move on to our next location."

"And what about this MacCandlish guy? What do we do about him?" he asks.

"If he becomes a chance target, so be it, we kill him, but we need to focus on creating havoc and killing as many western infidels as possible. That is our mission."

He looks at her and says, "Okay, let's get busy building more bombs. It's time to strike terror into the hearts of these Americans."

They get up from the small table in the kitchen area of the RV, and just as they are about to get back to business as usual, they hear a knock at their front door.

CHAPTER 46

TC is smiling. After three weeks of paperwork, including permits and releases, it looks like the process of searching for the buried pirate treasure can finally go forward.

Coastal Carolina University, the University of South Carolina, and Clemson University are all supplying students and faculty members for the project. Each university will have a sector to work. They will begin by using metal detectors over their sector and if the detector finds something, they will flag the location and other assigned students will carefully proceed to process the area to see if there is anything of value there.

Next, they will process each sector with a high-resolution ultrasound detector, which can penetrate the ground almost ten feet. Again, if something is located they will flag the area and a team of students will come in and carefully begin a "dig."

The first two weeks are frustrating. They have found nothing of value and everyone involved seems to be getting antsy and ready for something to happen. On the sixteenth day, they get their wish.

CHAPTER 47

Phil and Anna both look at each other and Phil puts his finger up to his lips. He quietly reaches into the small closet beside the kitchen and retrieves an AK-47 while Anna pulls her .38 from her purse. She carefully pulls the kitchen curtain away from the window and gazes outside. She quietly goes over to the kitchen table and writes a note, which she shows to Phil as the person knocks again. The note reads, RV office manager.

She puts her gun back in her purse and Phil places his assault rifle back in the closet as he backs away toward the bedroom where he pulls a handgun from the dresser.

Anna opens the door a crack and says, "Yes?"

He replies, "Sorry to disturb you, but the bug guys are coming next week on Wednesday and we will need to get in the RV to spray, and since I didn't have a phone number for you, I decided to stop by and let you know."

"No problem, just give us a heads up when you know the exact time."

He thanks her, turns away to leave but then turns back around and says, "Do you have a cell phone number so I can call you?"

Thinking quickly, she replies, "Sorry, we only have one and I dropped it in the ocean the other day and it is ruined. I'm getting a new one tomorrow, so I'll stop by the office and give you the number. I need to go. I have dinner cooking on the stove."

"Oh, no problem. That would be great, thanks again," he says as he turns and walks away.

Anna closes the door and breathes a sigh of relief. Phil walks out from the bedroom and says, "That gives us three days before we leave. Let's get busy."

*****

As Dave Dalton, the RV office manager and a retired cop from Charlotte, walks away, he senses something isn't right. When Anna first cracked open the door, he thought he smelled gunpowder and he did not smell or hear any food cooking in the RV directly behind her. With all the explosions going on and talk about terrorists, his senses have been heightened. He now needs to decide whether to call the local authorities or see if he can gather more information and maybe make one more arrest, which could be the biggest of his career.

Dalton has been in Myrtle Beach almost six months. His daughter, Martha lives nearby so he and his wife, Helen moved here to be closer to her. He wanted to get a job with a security company or private investigation company, but didn't have any luck so he took the job as office manager and security officer for the RV campground. They provided him a nice furnished doublewide to live in and a decent salary.

One of the PI companies he spoke with was Grand Strand Investigations in Cherry Grove. The owner, Mickke MacCandlish, told him that they were well staffed, but if they ever needed anyone, they would give him a call. When Dalton said he might start his own PI company, Mr. MacCandlish told him if he ever needed backup with a case, to let him know, they would be happy to oblige. He is now wondering if he should call Mr. MacCandlish about his gut feeling that there is a problem, because if he calls the police, he knows they will not let him in on the arrest. He figures Mr. MacCandlish may be willing to agree to allow him to help.

CHAPTER 48

I'm in my office with my feet up on my desk contemplating my next move. I keep trying to convince myself that I'm getting too old to run around the world and solve everyone's problems. Also, while in the custody of the DEA, Bob Linde confessed that the Valdez family hired him to get rid of me. I'm upset my Colombian friends sent someone else to kill me, and I'm highly pissed off that the terrorists came after my friends and not just me. Just as I am about to make a decision, my cell phone rings. The name looks familiar, so I take the call.

"Mr. MacCandlish, this is Dave Dalton. I talked to you a few months ago about a job with your company."

"Oh sure Dave, I remember you, from Charlotte. What can I do for you?"

Just as he is about to answer, Jim bursts into my office. "Dave, something just came up in the office. Can I call you right back?"

"Sure, but don't forget. It's important."

Jim blurts out, "A bomb just went off at the beach. No one was killed, but there are a lot of people hurt."

"What location?"

"Don't know, just somewhere along the beach."

"Thanks Jim, see what you can find out and keep me updated, and see if you can find Mark and update him as well."

"Will do," he says.

I dial the number on my phone and Mr. Dalton answers. We no more than begin our conversation when I notice Sam is calling me. "Sorry Dave, got another call I have to take. I'll call you right back."

Mr. Dalton is perplexed. What does he have to do to talk to someone about possible terrorists?

"Don't tell me, a bomb went off at the beach," I remark.

"Guess you're watching the news."

"No, Jim just came in and told me about it. What can we do to help?"

"Well, how about finding out who they are and where they are located. We seem to be at a dead end. There were no cameras near the explosion and it looks like a pipe bomb in a trash can."

"Okay detective, we'll hit the streets and see if we can find out anything. I'll keep you updated."

She hangs up without any further comment. The tone of her voice tells me she is frustrated.

After a few minutes of contemplation, I return my call to Mr. Dalton. "Sorry Mr. Dalton, a bomb just went off at the beach. Everyone seems to be in a tizzy right now."

"That's what I'm calling you about, Mr. MacCandlish. I may have a lead for you on the terrorists."

I can't believe what he just said. "I'm all ears, Mr. Dalton. What have you got?"

"Well, before I give you any details, I would like you to agree to let me tag along when you go to check out my information."

After a few seconds, I respond. "Tell you what I'll do. Tell me what you know and I'll make my decision based on that info. If it sounds worthy, of course you can tag along."

He fills me in about what he is thinking and what happened at the RV the other day. "Why did you wait a day to call?" I ask.

"I was debating whether to call you or the police. I wanted to be part of the take down and finally decided the police would not go along with that."

"So, give me a description? You said it was a man and a woman?"

He describes both suspects and the vehicle they are driving. They fit what I remember except his description of the woman is that she had blonde hair. The real kicker is that he also noticed two other men at the RV and they were driving a van. He also stated that he has not seen the other two men with the van in the last couple of days.

"So, Dave, do you know if they are there right now?"

"Not right now. I saw them leave about two hours ago and they haven't come back."

"What is your location? We'll be there right away. Whatever you do, don't go in on your own, okay?"

"No problem. I understand what backup is." He gives me the address and I give him my cell phone number just in case they get back before we get there.

CHAPTER 49

My next call is to Sam. "Detective, I may have a lead on the whereabouts of the terrorists. I just had a call from a guy who thinks they may be staying in an RV park."

She quickly replies, "Oh, my God, that's great. Give me the address and I'll have SWAT over there in a matter of minutes."

"Well, there is a problem. They are not there right now. Would you like to hear what I think you should do?"

"No, but I'll listen anyway."

"Since they are not there, I believe they are out placing more bombs around town. So why don't we go over there and cover the location, while you and all of your people hit the beach and the streets to try and catch them before they set off any more?"

There is silence on the other end. I'm beginning to think I've lost the call, until finally she says, "Too late, Mickke D, there was just another explosion at the beach. Pipe bomb, trash can."

"Damn. So what are you going to do?" I quickly ask.

"Give me the address, go over there and I'll send backup later. Just keep me advised," she replies.

"You got it. Good luck."

I grab two more clips from my desk drawer and run down the hallway to Jim's office. "Have you found Mark?"

"No, he must be out where there's no signal."

"Okay, we need to go. Do you remember Dave Dalton? He came in looking for a job about a month ago. He thinks the terrorists are staying in his RV park and Sam wants us to check it out. Bring all the ammo you have. Let's take your vehicle. They know mine. But we need to stop by mine. I put my M-16 in the back which may come in handy."

*****

Every police officer, including State Highway Patrolmen and Sheriff's deputies in Horry and Georgetown counties are out searching for the terrorists. They are at the beach and on the streets. They are particularly interested in areas where there are trash cans and no cameras. They have a description of the suspects and the car they are driving.

*****

Phil and Anna ditch the Impala and steal another car. They transfer all of the remaining pipe bombs to the new vehicle and look for new locations to wreak terror on the population of Myrtle Beach.

*****

We arrive at Mr. Dalton's without any problems. Jim knew exactly where it was. I didn't ask how he knew that. We park Jim's SUV in Mr. Dalton's driveway and go inside. I can't help but notice armored vests lying on the couch. "Are you expecting a war Dave?" I ask in a kidding manner.

"Well, you never know. Didn't know if you guys had any of these. Help yourself."

Without a second thought, Jim and I put one on. "Is there anyone else here with you?"

"No, I sent my wife over to our daughter's for the day."

"Do you have any kind of a map which shows the location of the RV you think they could be staying in?"

Without hesitation he replies, "I sure do. Take a look at this."

He shows us a site map, which shows every lot and RV location. The one he is referring to is at the far end, closest to the beach. The map also shows a fence between the park and the beach dunes.

"Dave, does that fence go all the way around the park?"

"Yes, it does. They have to come and go through here if they're driving a vehicle. However, there are several pedestrian gates which you can go through if you're walking to the beach."

I look at Jim. "I guess we should do a drive by and see if they've returned home. Dave, do you have a key to get in the RV?"

"Sure do. Let me get it."

He returns in seconds with the key and we get into Jim's vehicle. We drive slowly toward the end of the RV park. I tell Jim I want him to stop before we get to the location so we can have a look around before going in. Dave points and says, "There it is, that black one over there."

We are about 50 yards away and there isn't much going on around the suspect RV. "Dave, are any of those other RVs occupied?"

"No, the closest one is that blue one five lots away. All of the others are empty."

After a minute to gather my thoughts, I say, "Okay, here's what we are going to do. Dave, I want you to stay here and cover us. If you see any civilians coming this way, stop them. Jim and I are going in and see what we can find. Let me have the key."

Dave replies, "Be careful, it could be booby trapped."

I quickly say, "Yeah, I thought about that."

Jim has his .44 caliber pistol and I have my .45. I get in the trunk of Jim's vehicle and gather up my M-16, which was a gift from my commanding officer at Ft. Bragg, Colonel Townsend. Jim and I walk slowly toward the black RV. I'm not sure about these vests right now. They are bright blue and have POLICE written across the front. We are not going to sneak up on anyone with these on.

We reach the door of the RV without any problems. I look at Jim and nod my head. He places the key in the lock, turns it, and nothing happens. He tries it again with no success. He looks at me and whispers, "The bastards changed the locks."

"Okay, let's get back to the vehicle and wait around," I say.

We go quickly back to where Jim's parked and get back in his SUV. My heart rate finally begins to slow down as we ponder our next move.

CHAPTER 50

On the sixteenth day, at around 11 a.m., the Coastal Carolina students get a nice ping on their metal detectors. They flag the location and a second set of students begin to remove the topsoil to try to figure out what caused the metal detector to register. TC is in the area and comes over to check it out. After almost thirty minutes and nothing to show for their efforts, TC suggests they bring over the high-powered machine and take a look with it. After about twenty minutes of going back and forth over the location an image appears. He calls over the Coastal Carolina person in charge. "So, what do you think this is?"

"Not sure, but we are going to find out. It almost looks like a coffin." She gets on her phone and calls the dig crew over to begin the excavation of the location. Word spreads quickly among the students, and everyone migrates to the location. Just seconds after the crew arrives, she gets a call. She looks at TC, and sighs. She says to the dig crew, "Shut it down. We have to pack up and leave the area."

TC is dumbfounded. Somehow, the word "coffin" got back to the people in charge at Hobcaw Barony. If anyone discovers a burial site or cemetery, they need permits from the county and the state before going any further. Even though this may not be either of the above, they can't take any chances.

"So now what?" he asks.

"We file permits and wait until they are approved," she replies.

"And how long will that take?" he asks, frustrated.

"You never know, a week, a month, six months. Depends on who does the work."

"What can I do to speed things up?"

"Unless you know people in high places, there is not much you can do."

He thinks for a second, "Is the governor a high enough place?".

CHAPTER 51

Phil and Anna notice the uptick in law enforcement in the area and decide to shut things down for the day and wait for a day or two before finishing the job. Phil tells Anna to head back to the RV and he reminds her, “Be sure and remind me to turn off the alarm when we get in there.”

They wired an alarm system to a detonator when they first moved in, just in case someone tried to break into the RV. Ten seconds after entering the door, the RV will go up in a ball of flames if they do not turn the alarm off.

“No problem.”

*****

Dave hears a vehicle coming our way and looks out the back window. “Everyone duck, here they come. Different car, but that’s them.”

We hug the seats as the car slowly goes by. They stop at the end of the street and then cautiously turn into the small driveway next to the RV. All of a sudden, we need to decide if we should try to take them outside the RV or wait for them to get inside. I answer the question, “Okay guys, let’s do it and spread out. I doubt if they’re going to give up without a fight.”

We exit the car and my thoughts go to the movie “Gunfight at the OK Corral.” We are walking right at their vehicle with guns in hand. They must have spotted us, because, all of a sudden, the doors open, and a man and a woman scurry out of the vehicle. Both are armed and pointing weapons at us. The man fires, as the woman makes a dash for the RV.

"Get down and fire!" I yell. All three of us hit the grass and fire our weapons. Bullets are whizzing all around me as I slowly take aim with my M-16 at the man with the gun. Pop, pop, he goes down. I turn my attention to the woman who is now unlocking the door of the RV. She grabs her leg as either Dave or Jim hits their target. She is turning the lock and opening the door as I fire again. She falls through the front door of the RV.

Tick tock, tick tock. We slowly get up and walk toward the RV. Tick tock, tick tock. For some reason, I stop and hold my hand up. Jim and Dave stop as well. "What's wrong?" Jim asks.

Tick tock, tick tock. Ka-boom! The RV explodes in a ball of flames. We are all picked up and knocked to the ground by the force of the explosion. After what seems like an eternity, I pick my head up and look around. The car they drove up in is on fire and the RV is pretty much gone. I say, "Everyone okay?"

Jim answers, "I think so, but my ears and eyebrows can't take too many more of these."

"Dave, you okay?"

"I think so. Is this what retirement is all about? I'm going back to the Police Force. It wasn't nearly as dangerous."

We hear sirens coming our way. I tell everyone to drop their weapons and raise their hands. We don't want to get shot by friendly fire. The SWAT team bounds out of their vehicle with guns drawn. The same guy we met in Longs says, "Stand down." and the men lower their guns.

"Gentlemen, we need to stop meeting this way. Is everything under control?"

"Yes sir, I think they are both dead. One was outside near that car and the other was inside the RV when it exploded."

Sam arrives next, along with Woolever and Stratton. "Mickke D, you guys okay?"

"Yeah, I think so. But if we do this much more, we need to be on your payroll."

She gives me that are you kidding me look and moves on to talk with the SWAT team leader. She returns and staring directly at Jim, says, "You all need to come down to the station and write down what happened today. And by the way," looking at Dave, "who are you?"

"Dave Dalton, retired Charlotte police."

"Well Dave Dalton, retired Charlotte police, you should be there as well. I'll find out then how you got mixed up with these guys."

"No problem," he replies.

CHAPTER 52

It has been two weeks since Hobcaw filed the proper paperwork with the "powers that be" for the permits to dig up whatever might be there. TC decided not to contact the governor. He finally gets the call to meet everyone at the office the following day to go back to the dig site.

It seems like the shuttle takes forever to get to the site but finally they arrive. The site is almost 100 yards from the drop off place and TC is the first off the shuttle. He walks briskly toward the site, stops, looks down, and as everyone watches, he sits down in the grass next to the site and puts his head in his hands.

As the rest of the party arrives, they notice a mound of dirt next to the location. They look down into an empty hole. They see an old wooden ladder, some mud, bones, and the remains of some sort of a wooden box. Most of the students are excited about the bones, but TC is not one of them.

The supervisor in charge arrives, looks at the site, and says, "Oh, my God, what happened?"

TC looks at her and replies, "What does it look like happened? We've been robbed." After a short pause, he continues, "Can I speak to you in private?"

"Sure, let's go back to the shuttle." She looks at the students and barks an order, "Everyone cool it and don't touch anything. I'll be right back."

They walk in silence back to the shuttle. After sitting down, TC asks, "How could this have happened? Don't you have any security that could have prevented this?"

"I don't know. The gate is locked at night when we leave and everyone who comes in is with a guide."

TC looks at her and points. "What about the bay, do you have that covered as well?"

"Oh, my God, they came in by boat?" she exclaims. "Do you think it was an inside job, maybe one of the students?"

"I doubt it. They never knew what they were searching for. Do you mind if I bring my partner down to look around? He's a private investigator."

"No, I don't mind. Should we excavate what's left at the location?"

"No, let's wait until he gets here. I'm going to call him right now."

CHAPTER 53

Terror no longer grips the beach. It's been a week since the terror threat was removed. We all did our interview with Detective Concile and she thanked us in her own small, roundabout way.

The newspapers, radio, and TV stations have been having a ball second guessing law enforcement. Everyone is asking why a private investigator was involved with the demise of the terrorists. On the positive side, the publicity has been good for our business. We have seen an increase in calls coming into the office. Jim is not happy with that because it cuts into his golf time.

*****

I'm contemplating my next move and right now I have two choices. I would love to go down to Colombia and wipe out the Valdez cartel, which would hopefully stop people from that part of the world trying to kill me, but I also think I should go back to my hometown of Lancaster, Ohio, and see if I can figure out what happened to my old high school friend, Jake.

While I'm thinking, my cell phone rings. It's TC. "Mickke D, I have a job for you."

I yank his chain a little. "Hey TC, nice to hear from you and how are you doing today?"

"I need you down at Hobcaw Barony right away. We've been robbed."

There goes that we bit again. I haven't been robbed, at least not that I know of. I continue to pull his chain. "So I take it there has been a problem with finding the buried treasure?"

"Problem? You might say that. Someone came in while we were waiting for permits and took whatever was at the site. I believe it's all gone except for an old wooden box, some bones, and a lot of mud."

I think about it for a few seconds. It's hard to turn down anything that has to do with old buried pirate treasure, and TC knows that. "Okay, I'll be there in about an hour."

"Thanks Mickke D, I really appreciate this. I'll meet you up front in the reception area."

As I'm leaving the office, I ask Jannie to call up to Inlet View Bar & Grill in Shallotte Point, N.C., and make some dinner reservations for Saturday night. I want to take everyone in the office out to try to make up for the fact I almost got them all killed.

On my trip down to Georgetown, I continue to think about my next move, Colombia or Lancaster. I also am thinking about who would possibly want to steal the treasure from TC, and only one name keeps popping up. Stephanie Langchester.

As far as Colombia is concerned, I'm thinking, *I can't call Colonel Townsend again for help. He did more than his share the last time I went to Colombia and attacked the Valdez cartel. This time I will be on my own, although he may be able to get me the firepower I will need.*

As far as Lancaster is concerned, I'm not sure how to handle that. There was a lot going on in that cave and I almost died on that mountain. I'm not looking forward to climbing up there again, but I feel I owe it to Jake.

*****

I arrive 20 minutes late, and I can see TC pacing back and forth in front of the building as I pull up. He walks up to my vehicle and opens the door for me. "You must have run into traffic. You're late."

With a grin on my face, and while shaking his hand, I reply, "Not really. I just forgot how long it takes to get down here."

He points toward the shuttle and says, "Jump on the shuttle. It will take us to the location."

He goes over everything that has happened so far on the trip to the site. I can tell he is upset. He has not mentioned Stephanie, but I can tell she is on his mind. I beat him to the punch. "So who could possibly have done this other than your friend Stephanie?"

"She's not my friend, and I thought about that, but how could she have possibly known about it? There was no press, no TV, no radio, not a thing about what we were doing."

"She could have been following you. She's good. You would never have known."

I can tell the thought of that unsettles TC even more. He is quiet the rest of the ride to the site.

We arrive at the site, and the students and advisers are all waiting at the drop-off location. The Hobcaw Barony supervisor has decided to take everyone back to the reception area until we are finished.

TC leads me down to the site. Of course, the first thing I do is look out at the bay. The site is no more than 100 yards from the edge of the water. TC senses my thought process. "Yeah, it would be pretty easy to come in by boat, wouldn't it?"

"For someone with Stephanie's background, it would be a piece of cake. But, you know what? She couldn't do it alone. She would have needed help."

CHAPTER 54

Stephanie Langchester is a very creative person. Her background in marine biology and six years with British Intelligence served her well. She has been following TC for more than a month, and the last two weeks from a rented boat out in the bay watching everyone work on shore. She bought a mannequin from Flamingo Porch Consignment in Murrells Inlet, dressed it up to look like a fisherman, and sat it in a chair at the back of the boat. She hooked up a fishing rod to the dummy; from shore, you could not tell the difference. Occasionally, she would walk over and pretend to talk to "Barney," but most of the time she was watching the shore with binoculars from under the canopy.

She was on her boat the day the word came to shut the project down. She watched everyone leave, for no apparent reason. After all were gone, she took the boat up to the shoreline, got out, and took pictures of the site. She returned to her long-term rental in Georgetown, not quite sure of her next move. After going back out in the bay the following two days and seeing no activity on shore, she began making a list of what she would need: two shovels, a pickaxe, heavy-duty canvas bags, a cart for moving her bounty to the boat, a six-foot stepladder, and a tent to cover the site.

She considered hiring help but quickly decided against it. Too many cooks spoil the soup, and she would probably have to get rid of them in the end. Too many people have died already, so this time she would do it on her own. If something goes wrong, she will have no one to blame but herself.

She spent the next two days watching from the boat and what she saw made her very happy: nothing, nothing at all. The site is empty. They have shut it down. It is time for a practice run. She takes the boat out the following evening on a fishing trip with Barney. She goes on shore, walks up to the site and never sees anyone. She does notice swarms of mosquitoes, so the next day she picks up repellant, gloves and a long-sleeve shirt.

The following night, her adventure begins.

CHAPTER 55

TC and I decide to walk down to the bay. As we walk, I am looking down to see if I notice anything that might relate to a possible robbery. There had been quite a bit of rain in the area, hence the mud at the site. I notice what looks like two different sets of some kind of tire or cart tracks, one set without much depth and a second set that is fairly deep. The second set was hauling something heavy. I also noticed several footprints in the soft sandy soil not far from the water, as well as prints around the site itself. All of the footprints appear to be from the same person. I showed the tracks to TC. "TC, you see this set of tracks and footprints?"

"Yes, I do. And your point is?"

"That is your treasure being moved by Stephanie, or someone from the site on to a boat."

His eyes follow the tracks I am pointing to. "Damn, she robbed me again! First my boat and now the treasure!"

"Yeah, but at least, you got your boat back."

He rolls his eyes at me. "So, what can we do?"

There's that *we* bit again. "TC, we can't do anything unless you know where she went with the treasure, even if there was treasure. You don't even know that for sure."

TC looks around and turns to go back up to the site. "Well, you said she was hauling something heavy, didn't you? It wasn't dirt because she left the dirt here. I think we should look in the hole and see what we can find."

We return to the site and look down into the six-foot hole. There is mud, some bones, an old, decayed wooden stepladder, and what's left of some kind of a wooden box. I also notice something else. There are four fairly well-defined holes on each corner of the site. "TC, look. She had a tent over the site. She must have done this at night and didn't want anyone to see her lights. She thought this through real well."

He looks at me and says, "So, who's going down?"

I don't hesitate with my answer, "You are, my shoes are new."

He cautiously jumps down into the hole. Once there, he tries not to step on any of the bones. "TC, they're dead." I say. "Do what you have to do before someone comes down here and arrests us for grave robbing."

Looking up at me, he asks, "Do you have anything to dig with?"

"No, but you do, your hands and fingers. Get on with it."

After a couple of minutes of digging around in the mud, he finds a small bag. The bag is made of fabric and has a drawstring. He carefully opens the bag and I see him pull out a small piece of paper.

He reaches into the small bag and pulls out a gold ring and a small pearl necklace. He places everything back in the bag. I help him climb back out of the hole and he hands the bag to me.

I take the bag and say, "So what's in here? This is not from the 1700s."

He sits down in the grass and says, "Open it."

I open the bag and read the note. *Didn't want to take everything, TC, so I left you a couple of souvenirs. Tell Mickke D I can't wait to see him again.*

I laugh. "Now there's a woman with a huge set of balls."

TC is not laughing. He gets on his phone, calls Hobcaw, and asks them to send the shuttle back down to pick us up. He tells them that we are finished and the site is all theirs to do with whatever they wish. I ask him if he is going to tell them about the gift.

"No way. That belongs to me. It's not much, but it's better than nothing."

Whatever happened to the *we* bit now? Oh well, you win some and you lose some.

CHAPTER 56

It takes Stephanie Langchester four nights of hard work to dig the hole and recover the buried treasure. She takes Barney out in the boat every day to see if there is any activity at the site before making her night run. Each night she covers the site with a small tent so if anyone happens to be close by, they would not see any illumination coming from the headlamp attached to her ball cap. When she comes across the first glimpse of gold and silver, she actually begins to cry, but the tears quickly turn to joy and laughter. She has finally found it. She cannot believe her eyes.

Before making her final trip back to the boat with the last of the treasure, she laughs to herself and decides to leave TC a small gift. Actually, she just wants him to know that she beat him to the treasure and to let Mickke D know she beat him as well.

Back at her rental, she fills four large duffle bags with the bounty wrapped in bubble wrap to muffle any noise. She hires a large boat with a captain in Charleston and makes the trip to her final destination, Cancun. She changes her name, gets business cards made to show she is an antique dealer and collector, purchases a large home on a bluff overlooking the beach and builds a "safe room" in the basement where she keeps the treasure, selling it off little by little when she needs cash. Stephanie Langchester has finally retired.

CHAPTER 57

TC is depressed, but at least his search for the buried treasure is over. He can now move on to his next adventure, but I am still not sure in which direction I will be heading next, north or south.

After several days of contemplating, I think it would be in my best interest and the safety of my friends that I make one last trip back to Colombia. I call my former commanding officer at Fort Bragg, Colonel Townsend. "Colonel T, it's Mickke D."

"Mickke D, I should say how nice it is to hear from you, but every time you call, you seem to want something from me. What is it this time?"

"Well, I have had two more attempts on my life courtesy of our Colombian friends, so I am planning one last trip to Bogotá. Before you say anything, I am not asking for a plane and a small army to go with me."

"I am certainly glad of that. I am still trying to explain our last trip, which of course never took place. So what do you need?"

"I need some grenades and a couple of LAWs?"

"How about an APC as well?" he counters.

"No, I don't think so, wouldn't fit on the plane, but I could use a silencer for my M-16 and .45.

After a couple seconds of silence, he says, "So you're going in alone?"

"Yeah, no sense putting anyone else in danger. They want me so they're going to get me. Hopefully they're going to wish they had left me alone."

"I understand. Let me look into it and I'll get back to you. How soon do you need this?"

"No rush, I haven't got my ride finalized yet. Call me if you can make it work."

CHAPTER 58

I know of quite a few pilots who can do what I need done, but not many who will do what I need done. My mind goes back to the pilot who flew us into Colombia last time. I ran into him again in Antigua, that time under not so good circumstances. He had told me he was thinking about buying a bar called Ricky's Dockside in Little River. Now, every time I drive by, I wonder if he really did. I guess it's time to find out.

I pull in to Ricky's Dockside around 4:00 that same afternoon. I remember the original sign said Bar & Grill, but it now reads, Saloon. I opt to leave my .45 in my vehicle and when I get to the entrance, I see that I made a wise decision. There's a sign next to the door, "No Firearms, No Gang Colors, No Drugs." Then I notice why the name is now Saloon. There is a set of swinging saloon doors on the front entrance. How cool is that?

I walk inside and notice several pool tables and about 20 people, some playing pool and others enjoying an adult beverage. I look around and see my pilot Rick seated at the bar.

He is staring into the mirror behind the bar and as I step inside, he says without turning, "Well, if it isn't Mickke D. I was hoping you would stop by. Hope you read the sign on the door about no firearms."

The bar immediately goes silent. The pool players stop playing and the adult beverage partakers stop drinking and everyone turns to face me. They all have a look on their faces that lets me know they are either ex-military or ex-CIA like Rick. One of the more husky pool players looks at Rick and says, "Is this the guy you were telling us about?"

Rick turns and with his usual big smile says, "Yeah, that's him. Mickke D, what can I do for you?"

I look around the room and think to myself, I hope they all read the sign on the door as well. "Can I talk to you outside?"

"Absolutely." He walks over, shakes my hand and leads me out through the old swinging saloon doors.

"Love those doors, Rick."

"Yeah, everyone thinks they're walking into an old wild West saloon. Now what can I do for you?"

After sitting down in a couple of rocking chairs facing Highway 17, I ask, "Are you still doing that pilot thing?"

"Not really, I sold the plane once I left the Bahamas and landed here. I used the money to buy the bar and a boat. I haven't flown anything since. Why do you ask?"

"Well, I need to make another trip to Bogotá and I'm looking for a ride."

"Why are you going back? Valdez is dead."

"I know, but someone from the Valdez cartel keeps trying to kill me. They have made two attempts on my life since I eliminated Valdez, one while I was in Antigua and another not too long ago at my house."

"Yeah, I remember that one in Antigua. We were flying over that one when it happened. Word is the wife and oldest son have taken over the reins of the cartel. If someone tried to take you out, the orders had to come from one of them."

"So you still have contacts in that part of the world?" I ask.

He smiles. "Mickke D, I have contacts all over the world and so do most of the people in the bar right now."

After a slight pause while I try to digest that statement, I continue, "So would you be interested in a trip to Bogotá?"

His smile disappears. "I just told you, I don't have a plane anymore."

"That's no problem. I'll furnish the plane and pay you 10K for flying me there.

"Who else is going? Is that Mark guy going? I don't think he likes me."

"No, Mark isn't going. It will just be you and me."

His smile disappears again, and his eyes widen. "Are you crazy? I'm just the pilot. That leaves you to do the dirty work."

"That's right. All you have to do is fly the plane."

After a pause he asks, "When do you have to know?"

"No rush. Here's my card. Think about it and give me a call."

"Thanks." Without saying anything more, he turns and goes back through those swinging doors and into the saloon. I notice the low roar of people talking and drinking suddenly becomes mute as Rick enters the building.

*****

I start to form a plan in my head. Since I did not get an absolute "no" from Rick, I figure my odds are at least 50-50 he will decide to go.

When I get back to the house and after taking Blue for a walk, I begin to write down where I need to go, what I need to do, and how long it should take me to accomplish my task.

Around 7:00, my phone rings. "Colonel T, do you have any good news for me?"

"Mickke D, one of these days your extracurricular activities are going to cause me to lose my silver oak leaves. I hope it's not this time. I can get you three LAWS, six grenades, and the silencers you asked for. Where can we meet? Whatever you do, make it a private location. I don't need to get arrested for arms peddling."

"Thanks, but I still haven't sewed up my ride yet. I should know soon. I'll call you back one way or the other and again, thank you."

I go to bed early but I don't get a lot of sleep because I keep going over in my mind what happened on my last trip to Bogotá. I wonder if everything is the same as it was that time, or if they improved their security around the compound. I guess I'll find out when and if I get there.

Blue wakes me up around 7 a.m. the following morning wanting to go out, and all of a sudden, today I feel more like a soldier than a civilian. My normally mellow demons are beginning to awaken in my belly. I know the feeling, and it is not a good one.

CHAPTER 59

Early Saturday morning, two days after making my appeal to Rick, he calls me back. "Can you come down to the bar around ten this morning?"

"I'll be there," I quickly reply.

I arrive about 9:50 and notice three vehicles parked outside the bar. I remember the sign on the door said hours were 11:00 until closing on Saturdays. I'm getting that itchy feeling which seems to go with my soldier mood lately but if I were being set up, I doubt if it would be this obvious.

After a short debate with myself, I take my weapon with me, and walk up to the old swinging saloon doors. I carefully push the doors open and walk in. Rick and two other gentlemen are seated at one of the tables in the room.

"Come on in, Mickke D. I want you to meet a couple of friends of mine. This is Harley and this is Bos."

I shake their hands and notice both men as well as Rick are also carrying. Rick grins. "The sign only pertains to business hours. I've decided to take you up on your offer to fly you to Bogotá, and since Harley and Bos don't like what the Valdez cartel does anymore than you and I, they would like to come along and help you out."

I look closely at Harley and Bos. Both are probably in their mid-50s and look like they're in pretty good shape although Bos is short in the hair department. "Gentlemen, what are your backgrounds?"

Harley answers first. "Retired Army Ranger."

Bos responds, "Retired CIA. What is your background?"

I know they already know the answer, but I answer anyway, "Special Forces."

With a very benign look, Harley quickly retorts, "No problem, we won't hold that against you."

I give them a half-ass smile as Rick looks at me and begins the conversation. "Harley and Bos want 5K each and we all want our money up front. You provide the plane, and Harley and Bos will provide their own weapons. We fly in, do the job and get out. By the way, what are you planning on doing once we get there?"

"I plan to blow up the compound and the helicopter if it's there. Why would you guys want to go along, except for the money?"

"We both spent time there and we know what happens in that part of the world." Harley replies, "We also know what happens to the people who end up with the coke here in the States. If we can do anything to slow things down, we will do it."

"If we go, what will we be facing security wise once we get there?" Bos asks.

"Not sure. Rick says, you have contacts all over the world. See if you can find that out, and I'll let you know if I want company."

Bos looks at Rick and then just shrugs his shoulders. "We can do that."

I look at Rick. "So what do we need plane wise?"

"I've been thinking about that. We need an Aerostar 702P which is a 702 modified with auxiliary fuel tanks. She'll cruise at 260 knots and one fuel stop in Panama will be all we need. We'll need to stop in Florida on the way back for fuel."

"Okay, call me with the info on the plane and who I need to contact. I'll get your plane. See what you can find out about security at the compound." Looking at all three, I continue, "I want to do this ASAP."

All three of them nod their heads. I get up, shake hands with everyone and leave the saloon.

Once I get back home, I call Colonel Townsend. "Colonel T, I've got a pilot and a plane."

"Great, who is the pilot?"

"Do you remember Rick, our pilot on our first trip to Bogotá? Well, I ran into him again when I was in Antigua and he actually ended up buying a bar in Little River, not far from where I live. He has agreed to fly me there. Where would you like to meet me with the weapons?"

"You know Mickke D, I have some leave time available. Maybe I'll go on that trip with you."

I am dumbfounded. "Are you sure about that? This could be a one-way trip."

"Well, I figure if I go along, maybe I can help you get it right this time, and then you won't be calling me every six months for backup, Pops," he jokes, referencing a young lady friend of mine.

"Very funny. Let me think about this for a while. I'll get back to you."

"No problem. You have my number."

I'm not sure what to think about this. I've spent a lot of time around Colonel Townsend, but I've never been on a mission with him.

CHAPTER 60

That same night, I take Jim, Mark, and Jannie to dinner at Inlet View Bar & Grill in Shallotte Point, N.C. On the ride up, I tell them the evening is my treat to show my appreciation for their hard work and to apologize for almost getting them blown up.

Mark laughs. "It wasn't the first time and probably won't be the last." Everyone laughs but Jannie. She just gives all three of us a strange look.

I've always enjoyed Inlet View with its great food and fantastic vistas. I try to keep the atmosphere and conversation as light as possible, but I keep thinking this may be the last time we all have dinner together.

We end up with a very good waitress. She introduces herself as Margaret, but she says to call her Maggie. She is from the U.K. and has a great accent. We ask her how she ended up over here and she says she came to visit her son Chris, and liked it so well, she decided to stay. We all welcome her to the beach.

I ask her, "Did you ever know a woman by the name of Stephanie Langchester who was also from the U.K.?"

I notice a slight change in her expression but she replies without blinking an eye, "No, the name does not sound familiar."

Later on, Samantha Hughes, the owner, stops by and asks us if everything is all right. We reply we are having a great time, our dinner was fantastic and we really enjoy Maggie, our waitress. She tells us to ask her how she got the nickname Dobber Dowde.

Jannie asks that question when Maggie returns. She looks around and replies, "It sounds like Samantha has been telling tales out of school." She then gives us a half-smile and whispers, "If I told you that, I would have to kill all of you."

We are all speechless, and then she gives us a hearty laugh. "Just a little English humor, folks!" She never answers the question.

We thank Maggie for a wonderful evening and I leave her a big tip and my PI business card, which I notice seems to get her attention.

Our conversation is minimal on the trip back. It's as if everyone knows something is not right.

One of us should have asked Maggie what she did back in the U.K. before she came over here. If we had, we probably would have got the same answer she whispered before: If I told you that, I would have to kill all of you.

Margaret Kemp studies the business card she got from Mickke D and thinks to herself, you were a lot easier to find than I thought you might be. That same evening, she makes a phone call to an old work acquaintance of hers up in Ohio.

CHAPTER 61

Two days later, Rick calls and says he is having a problem finding an Aerostar 702P to lease. He also reiterates the Aerostar is still the best plane for the job. Finally, after some hesitation, I say, "Okay, how much would it cost to purchase one?"

Rick is speechless for a few seconds and then replies, "You're kidding. You want to buy a plane for a one-day trip?"

My mind is searching for a plausible answer. "Well, I've always thought it would be nice to own a plane. I guess an Aerostar will work as well as any other. You're the expert. Find one that sounds good and we'll go take a look at it."

He hesitates, "You're serious, aren't you? I always thought you were one crazy bastard. Now I'm sure of it. Okay, let me do some checking around and I'll give you a call when I find one."

"Great Rick, get on it. Time is of the essence."

As I put my phone down, I say to no one in particular, "Great, just what I need, a freaking airplane, but if that's what it takes, so be it."

Thirty minutes later, Rick calls back. "Okay, I found a nice 1984 700P with less than 1,500 hours on it in Michigan for $350,000. The owner said he would fly it down here tomorrow if you're serious."

"I'm serious. Tell him to come on down. How about the Grand Strand Airport. Does that work?"

"No problem. I know the head guy over there. Consider it done."

The following day, with Rick at the controls, me in the co-pilots seat and the owner, Mr. Hazelton in the back, we take the Aerostar for a spin. Rick was right. This is one sweet ride. After we return from the flight, I sit down with the owner and we agree to a cash price of $335,000. Mr. Hazelton and I go to my bank and we complete the deal. I pay for a one-way ticket for Mr. Hazelton back to Michigan and Rick makes a deal to keep the plane at the airport. By 5:00 that afternoon, I own an airplane.

That night I call Colonel T and tell him I'm ready to go and is he sure he wants to tag along. He says yes. I ask him to come down to the beach. He can stay at my place and we can meet with Rick and the other two guys who want to go along. I would like his thoughts on Harley and Bos. He tells me he'll be here tomorrow by 10:00. I call Rick and ask him to set up a meeting with everyone around 11:00. I don't tell him I'm bringing company.

CHAPTER 62

Colonel T is late. He doesn't arrive until 10:05. He said he ran into a detour and couldn't make up the lost time. I just shake my head and smile.

I have never seen Colonel T in anything but an Army uniform but today, he is dressed in blue jeans, an Army T-shirt and tennis shoes. Tennis shoes? I actually thought he was born with combat boots on his feet.

He notices me looking at his attire and says, "Hey Pops, I'm on vacation."

I take that to mean, don't make fun of me and I won't make fun of you. I get the message loud and clear.

We get his gear squared away in the spare bedroom, have a cold beer, and then I call Rick to tell him we're on our way.

Colonel T says he will drive since my arsenal is in his trunk and he doesn't want to leave it unguarded. I agree and we head off to Ricky's. I grab my .45 and stick in my back holster.

"Damn Mickke D, we're just going to a meeting, not a shootout."

"Yeah, I know but when you have people constantly trying to kill you, you always come prepared."

"Do you mind if I leave mine in the car?"

"No problem," I reply.

On the way, I tell Colonel T about the fact that Harley and Bos both want 5K each to go along. He asks, "So they're paid mercenaries?"

I reply, "I guess. I have no problem paying Rick to fly the plane, but I'm not sure about the other two."

As we pull into the parking lot at 11:00, I notice several cars in the lot but the front door along with the swinging saloon doors are closed. I say to Colonel T, "I don't like the looks of this."

"My God, Mickke D, I just get into town and already you're getting me in to trouble. Why do you think there's a problem?"

"Every time I've been here during business hours, the front door has always been open and he opens at 11.

"Personally, I think you're paranoid."

"Better paranoid than dead," I respond.

"So, what are we doing, staying here or going in?" he asks.

"I'm going to call Rick." After several rings, the phone goes to voicemail.

I look at Colonel T. "He doesn't answer. Now I really think there's a problem."

Our attention turns to a car as it enters the parking lot and pulls up right in front of the door. A man gets out, walks up to the door, then turns and goes back to his vehicle. He starts the car, backs out and as he approaches our vehicle, I open my window and wave. The man stops and looks my way. I ask, "Is the bar closed?"

"Yeah, I guess so. There's a closed sign on the door."

I reply, "Thanks," and he continues on his way.

Colonel T says, "Maybe he's closed for the meeting."

"Or maybe there is a problem."

"Well, Mickke D, you're in charge. What do you want to do?"

Before I have a chance to answer, we hear a gunshot. I look at Colonel T and say, “I think it’s time you get your weapon out of the trunk.”

“I think you’re right,” he replies as he pops the trunk and moves to the rear of his vehicle.

Within seconds, we are walking toward the front door with weapons drawn. As we get to the door, we hear yelling from inside. I motion for Colonel T to cover one side of the door and I’ll cover the other.

We don’t have to wait long. The door opens and two rather unsavory looking individuals back out of the swinging doors, with guns in hand. They stop as they hear the sound of our weapons being cocked. They drop their weapons as they feel cold steel gun barrels against their ears.

We push them back in the bar and as I see Rick, I ask, “Is everyone okay?”

“We’re fine. These bastards robbed me and shot a hole in my ceiling. Can you believe that?”

“No, not really. Do you want me to call the cops?”

Rick finally notices Colonel T. “Colonel Townsend. What are you doing here?”

“Hey Rick. Mickke D invited me along on his trip. I hear you are going to fly us there.”

Rick looks at Harley and Bos and then back at us. “Why don’t you two wait out in the car while we have a talk with our robber friends here. Give us about fifteen minutes and then call the cops.”

“No problem,” I answer, but someone else must have already called the cops because here they come in full force. And as you can guess, Detective Concile is the first one out of the lead vehicle.

"Well, well, well, if it isn't Mickke D." And while looking at Woolever and Stratton, she continues, "Why should this surprise me?" They both shrug their shoulders.

"Detective Concile, I was just getting ready to call you. My friend and I were just stopping in for a cold one when we happened on a robbery in progress. We figured we would see if we could help. Robbery stopped. No one hurt. Perfect ending."

Looking directly at me, she replies, "Why do I think you're full of BS? Who is your friend, and does he have a permit to carry?"

Colonel T gets his wallet and hands his Army ID to Sam. She looks at Colonel T and at the ID and says, "And why should this surprise me either. Thank you Colonel Townsend. I'm not even going to ask you how you know him," pointing at me.

Rick hears the conversation and intervenes. "That's right, detective. If these guys had not stopped by, those guys would have been long gone with my money."

Rolling her eyes, she asks, "And who might you be?"

"I'm Rick Gibson. I own the place."

Shaking her head, she says, "Okay. Mickke D and Colonel Townsend, you're free to go after giving a statement to Woolever and Stratton. Rick, I need a statement from you as well," and looking at a couple of uniformed officers she continues, "Cuff these two, read them their rights, and take them to jail."

Rick exclaims, "Can I get my money first?"

"No, Rick, you may not get your money first. That's evidence. Once everything has been processed, you may then get your money."

Looking at Sam, I say, "You don't mind if we stay and have that cold one, do you? You're more than welcome to join us."

She just turns and walks away. Outside there is no smile but inside she is laughing. She just loves to pull Mickke D's chain.

Once the excitement is over, statements given, and everyone leaves, we finally sit down with Rick, Harley, Bos and a cold beer. Colonel T does not beat around the bush, "So you two are the paid mercenaries?" looking directly at Harley and Bos, "I hope you work better in the field than you did in here."

"They walked in the door with guns drawn. What did you expect us to do? And what are you talking about, paid mercenaries?"

"Well, I don't know. You want 5K a piece to go to Bogotá to get rid of some cartel bad guys, and you both say you hate these guys. Isn't that right?"

Harley responds, "That's about it, however, that doesn't necessarily make us paid mercenaries. That just means we want paid for services rendered."

"Good, that's fine with me. If Mickke D wants to pay you, so be it."

Without agreeing to anything, I say, "So has anyone been able to figure out if the security at the compound has changed since I was there last?"

Bos answers, "I contacted a friend of mine who is in the area and he said since the Panama government confiscated the jet belonging to the Valdez cartel, they are doing everything by helicopter. They now have two copters and both are located within the compound walls. The airstrip is now abandoned and the lights removed. The guard barracks is now located at the front gate of the compound. Only one guard mans the guard shack at the airstrip, and it operates as an exterior lookout post. They still have their roaming guards every two hours along with two guards at the front gate coming in the main road."

Rick jumps in, "No landing lights? I hope we're going in during the day."

After thinking for a few seconds, I respond, "I guess we go in during a full moon and hope it's not overcast and cloudy. By the way Rick, can you land our plane without the engines running?"

"Say what? Are you nuts?" he exclaims.

I look at Rick and reply, "We need to surprise them. Can you do it?"

Rick gets up and starts pacing around the bar. Finally he responds, "Probably, if we have a really bright moon, no wind, and a lot of luck."

I smile, "Great, it's settled. We go in during a full moon and everyone crosses their fingers, toes, and anything else they may want to try and cross. I'll get back to you with who's going along and when we're going. Thank you, gentlemen. Rick, can I see you outside?"

Once outside I say to Rick, "I need Harley and Bos's full real names and not any aliases."

"Sure, Harley Richards and Bos Jones."

"Thanks Rick, we'll be in touch."

"No problem. Thanks again for helping out today."

We both wave as we return to our vehicle.

CHAPTER 63

As soon as we get back to the house, I call Jim. "I figured you would be on the golf course. Have you got a minute?"

"Sure boss. I played early this morning. Hey, did I see Colonel Townsend over there today? Looked like him going up to your door when I pulled in."

He caught me off guard. After a second of silence, I reply, "Yeah, he's on vacation and I invited him to come down for a few days. I thought we might talk TC into taking us fishing and on a cruise around the area."

"Cool. Tell him I said hello. Now, what do you need?"

"I need you to check with your people on a couple of guys. Harley Richards and Bos Jones. The sooner the better. Harley is an ex-Army Ranger and Bos is ex-CIA."

"Does it have to do anything to do with Colonel Townsend being here?"

"Could be, but keep it under your hat. It's an ongoing investigation."

"You got it." He ends the call.

*****

"So what do you think of Harley and Bos?" I ask Colonel T.

"I think they're legit. I don't like the idea of contacting someone on the ground in Bogotá, but that's just me."

"Yeah, I don't like that, either. Someone may put two and two together." After a few seconds, I continue, "So where would you like to go for dinner tonight?"

"Up to you. You know the area a lot better than me."

"Okay, let's go to Boardwalk Billy's. Good food, nice atmosphere. I'm buying."

He quirks, "There is no doubt in my military mind that you're buying."

Halfway through dinner, Jim calls. "Hey boss, both of them check out fine. No problems. Anything else?"

"Thanks, Jim. That will do it for now."

We finish our dinner and head back to the house. I get on the computer and Google phases of the moon over South America. It looks like we go on Monday or Tuesday.

CHAPTER 64

I decide to take Harley and Bos along. We may need all the firepower we can muster. I call Rick and tell him to contact Harley and Bos and tell them they're in and I need bank account numbers to deposit their money. Rick hesitates and then replies, "Harley, Bos, and I have decided we will wait until we get back to get our money. Is that all right with you?"

This time I hesitate, "Sure, sounds fine to me. We go in Monday night. It will be a full moon and looks like clear skies over the compound. Does that work for everyone?"

"One day is as good as another. What time do we meet you at the airport?"

"Let's meet Monday morning at 9 a.m. and wear normal clothes to the airport. We'll change in Panama. Do you have to file a flight plan?"

"Yeah, but I'll fudge it. Don't worry."

"Hey, tell Harley and Bos to bring everything they have weapon and ammo wise. You never know what we may run into."

"No problem. See you at the airport."

*****

Along with Colonel T, I spend most of Sunday cleaning weapons and getting my shit together for the trip. I take time to type out a short will on the computer and ask Colonel T to witness it.

"Damn, Mickke D, you're not giving me a very positive feeling about this trip. It sounds simple enough to me. We land, blow up the main house at the compound along with the copters, and leave."

"I know. It sounds too simple. I hope it ends up that way."

I make a call to the office and leave a message that I won't be in until Wednesday. I say I have company in town. Jim will be able to verify that.

Sunday evening, I take Colonel T to dinner at The Parson's Table in Little River. We both enjoy our slow roasted prime rib dinner with a bottle of DeLoach Cabernet. While there, I go over our game plan for the attack.

The remainder of the evening is quiet and we both go to bed early. I don't know about him, but I have a hard time falling asleep. I keep thinking about all of the things that can go wrong. Thank goodness, my sleep proceeds without my recurring nightmares from the past.

CHAPTER 65

Everyone arrives 20 to 30 minutes early carrying duffel bags filled with a change of clothes and weapons. Our plane is still in the hanger, which makes it easier to load everything on board without roving eyes checking on us. There seems to be plenty of room to stow all of the baggage onboard. Rick uses a handheld scale to weigh everything and determines total weight seems to comply with weight limits for the AeroStar. We leave the airport right on schedule and head southwest to Panama.

The plane is a real jewel and doesn't seem to labor with all the weight onboard. I brought along a cooler with sandwiches and water for the trip down and another cooler with beer for the trip back. I sure hope we get to the cooler with the beer.

I hand everyone a radio for communication with each other and I give everyone a rough sketch of the compound as I remember. Colonel T and I go over our plan of action with Harley and Bos and they seem to confer with our assessment and game plan. Our main ploy is to eliminate the guard at the old guard shack at the airstrip before he can contact the main guard shack and the main house.

Our plan is to touch down around 0300 and leave by 0400. I hope we can get in and out while the roving guards are out on patrol and before the guards at the guardhouse on the road leading into the compound can react. The only unanswered question is how many guards will there be at the main guard house at the gated entrance of the compound. If it happens to be during a shift change, there could be five or six more guards than usual.

Thank goodness, Colonel T brought along four LAWS (light anti-armor weapon) instead of just two. I plan to use one LAW on the main house, and, if need be, one on the main guardhouse at the entrance. If that one is not needed, I'll use both on the main house. That will leave two for the copters. As a last resort, we'll use the grenades and small arms fire on the copters, hopefully enough to at least cripple the rotor blades so they can't fly.

The first 30 minutes of the flight is full of conversation and banter, but then we all get quiet and try to catch some shuteye. The realization of the trip is setting in, and everyone knows it could be his last rodeo. It's time to make final preparations.

About an hour before landing in Panama, Rick and Colonel T both make calls to the airport. Rick gets clearance to land and Colonel T secures an available private hanger where we can conceal the plane. We can change clothes and get our weapons ready for our final assault on the compound.

We arrive at the airport just before 11:00 p.m. local time. Rick has the plane filled with petrol while I go to the fuel office and pay the bill. I enter the office and go up to the counter where a very attractive young lady with dark hair is smiling at me. She asks, in perfect English if she can help me and I reply, "I would like to pay for the fuel you just put in to that AeroStar out there," pointing to our plane.

She pushes some keys on her computer and says, "That will be $615. May I have your credit card, please?"

I give her my best wish I had more time smile and reply, while gazing at her nametag, "Rosanne, I would like to pay in cash," as I pull my money clip from my pocket.

She gives me a strange look and finally says okay. I notice her hand disappear slowly under the counter, and then quickly return. She takes my money and hands me a receipt. "Would you like this made out to you or a company?"

"Neither. That is fine just like it is." I turn and leave the office.

Rick taxis the plane into the private hanger. We all get out and stretch our legs, eat some sandwiches and change our clothes. All is going according to schedule. That is until a Panamanian jeep and a truckload of soldiers pull up in front of the hanger. I immediately say to Colonel T, "This is not good."

"No shit," he replies, as the soldiers disembark with weapons at the ready.

"Any idea what this is about?" I say to Rick.

"Hell no, but someone had better have a good story for why we have all of these weapons."

Colonel T jumps in, "Let me handle this."

With hands raised, he walks over to the jeep where a soldier with braids all over his sleeves gets out and asks in broken English, "I am Major Ortega. Who are you, why are you here, and why do you have all of those weapons?"

Half-whispering, Colonel T replies as he shows him his Army ID, "I'm Colonel Townsend with U.S. Army Special Forces, and we are here for a special jungle training mission. You weren't notified we were coming?"

Looking almost embarrassed, he says, “Special Forces, huh. Sure, I was notified. I need to call my superior and tell him you have arrived. Wait here.”

Before he can turn away, Colonel T continues, “Major Ortega. I wouldn’t do that. This is supposed to be a secret mission and we are on a tight schedule. If we don’t get on our way, the mission will be a failure. Why don’t we just get back on our plane and continue on our way. I will make sure that your superiors know how helpful you were after the mission is over.”

Colonel T can tell he is thinking about that last statement. Major Ortega looks around and then motions for his men to get back on the truck. “Be sure and let my superiors know I was very helpful, Colonel, and good luck with your training.”

He salutes Colonel T and shakes his hand. We watch as the jeep and truck move out. Colonel Townsend yells out as he trots back to the plane, “Get back on the plane and let’s get the hell out of here.”

CHAPTER 66

Once in the air, we all breathe again. However, Rick quickly reminds us, “Hey, if they put up a fighter, we’re toast.”

After about 30 minutes, we finally feel safe again, but now we’re going to be two hours early. We’re going to arrive about 1:00 a.m. instead of 3:00 a.m.

Rick slows down the plane a bit and it looks like a 1:15 arrival. We go over the plan again and even add a Plan B and Plan C. We hope to avoid using them.

As soon as we get close to Colombian air space, Rick takes the plane down on the deck and under radar. We turn and head toward the compound. The sky is clear with a brilliant full moon, but this could be the scariest part of the entire mission.

Within what seems like only a few minutes, Rick says, “Okay guys, hold on. I’m going to shut her down. The trees are going to make it hard to see what’s left of the runway, so I’m going to turn the running lights on for a few seconds just to get us lined up. Let’s hope the guard is looking the other way.”

We feel the plane lose altitude as Rick turns off the engines and it begins to waver from side to side. He then hits the lights and we all see the runway in front of us. However, there is one big problem. There is a huge limb lying on the runway near the end where we are planning to land.

Rick exclaims, “Damn, we can’t hit that!” He pulls the nose up a tad bit and just barely clips the branch with the plane’s wheels. He then turns off the lights, touches down with a thud, and hits the brakes. The plane begins to slow down as we see the guard shack coming up on the right. Thank God, it is a long runway, built for the cartel's jet.

The plane comes to a stop about 100 yards short of the guard shack, and everyone in the plane finally takes a breath of air. We see no activity from the shack. I motion for Rick to open the door, and Colonel T and I climb out of the plane and disappear into the trees. We stay in the tree line and advance toward the guard shack.

Harley and Bos get off and jog back up the runway. They are going to try to pull the branch off the tarmac, because we will need to take off from that end of the runway.

Colonel T and I stop when we get to within 50 feet of the guard shack. We see no activity, but we do hear music. I motion for him to go around the back and I'm going to the front. I am having a hard time getting used to giving Colonel T orders. He was always giving me orders before, and I am finding the whole situation rather difficult. As he disappears around the building, I slowly reach the window and carefully gaze in. The guard is asleep in his chair. I doubt if he could have heard us over the sound of the music. With gun in hand and silencer in place, I slowly open the door and walk inside. I point my gun at the soldier but can't seem to pull the trigger.

All of a sudden, he opens his eyes and reaches for his weapon. I hear the sound of a silenced gunshot over my right shoulder. The soldier slumps in his chair. He will not be calling anyone to say we have arrived. I turn as Colonel T says, "Losing your edge, Mickke D? This is not the time for that. Let's move on."

I reply, "I had it," and move quickly out the door and toward a four-wheeler parked out front. I get on the radio and call Harley and Bos. "The guard is down and we are going in. We're taking a 4x4 and there's another one here for you guys. Are you ready?"

I recognize Harley's voice, "Yeah. We're just working on getting the limb off the runway and then heading back to the plane."

Colonel T pulls a muffler sound suppresser from his backpack and hands it to me. It looks like the same one he gave us on our initial visit here. I smirk and jam it on the muffler pipe. He hands me a second one and I place it on the second 4x4.

I get back on the radio, "Left you a noise suppresser on the seat of the 4x4. Stick it on the muffler pipe."

"Roger that."

I jump in behind the wheel and Colonel T takes the passenger seat with his M-16 at the ready. The four LAWS are on the back seat. The full moon makes the trail back to the compound easy to navigate. As we get closer, we can make out the lights on the wall facing out away from the main house. We are about to leave the concealed confines of the jungle and are heading into a cleared open area.

I stop and look at Colonel T. "They have to have added cameras on that wall. Let's ditch the 4x4 and get close to the wall. What do you think?"

"I think you're right. Grab two LAWS and I'll get the other two."

I get back on the radio and whisper, "We're ditching the 4x4 and going in along the wall. Believe they have cameras. Wait at our 4x4 until we blow the guard house and then move on up."

"Roger that."

Harley and Bos arrive back at the plane. Rick is standing outside with weapon in hand. He says, "Call me as soon as you start back. I'll fire her up and we'll be ready to get out of here. It's way too quiet. I don't like this."

He no more than finishes his sentence when several men step out of the tree line with weapons drawn and pointed. They converge on the plane.

Rick automatically hits the voice key on his radio four times, which is the code for we're in deep shit. He then nods at Harley and Bos to let them know what he has done. All three men drop their weapons and raise their hands.

CHAPTER 67

Just as we get to the wall, we both hear the code at the same time. I whisper, “Damn, there’s a problem at the plane.”

Colonel T whispers back, “I think you’re right. Let’s head back. No, I’ll head back. You blow the guard house and we’ll catch up with you.”

“Are you sure?”

“I’ll handle it. Go blow the guard house.” He hands me his two LAWS and trots back toward the 4x4.

I now am carrying four LAWS, three grenades, an M-16, and my .45, plus ammo. I think I should have gotten in better shape before I decided to do this.

*****

Colonel T navigates the 4x4 along the path until he catches a glimpse of the lights on the guard shack. At that point, he gets off the 4x4 and moves forward on foot, staying just inside the tree line. He finally gets close enough to see the problem.

Rick, Harley, and Bos are standing next to the plane with hands raised. There are two pods of security guards around them, four on the left and three on the right. He lays prone on the ground and lines up the first guard on the left. His silencer spits out the round and the guard drops. He fires again and the first guard on the right falls as well.

The other guards are dumbfounded and for the slightest moment, they turn and look behind them. Harley, Bos and Rick seize the opportunity, bend over, grab their ankle weapons, and fire at the remaining guards who all of a sudden are in limbo. Colonel T sees one remaining guard with rifle pointed at Rick and sends him to the ground. The guards never get off a shot and all are either dead or badly wounded.

Harley, Bos and Rick do not have silencers on their weapons and for about one minute, it sounded like a war zone. Colonel T runs over to the plane and checks that everyone is okay. He then tells Harley and Bos that they all need to get back to the compound and back up Mickke D.

Rick gathers up all of the weapons and tosses them into the jungle. He retains two AK-47s, which he keeps with him in case he has company before the guys return. He is alone to guard the plane.

*****

I hear the gunfire as I ease myself along the compound wall toward the guardhouse. So much for the element of surprise, I think to myself. Then reality sets in. What if Colonel T, Harley, Bos and Rick are dead? What if I'm out here alone with no backup? Then I remember, never allow negativity to set in while you are on a mission. I stop, take a deep breath and change my attitude. Finish the mission and if it's my last stand, then I will take a lot of bad guys along with me.

I proceed along the wall until I can see the road leading into the main compound gate. I don't hear any more gunfire or any new sounds coming from the compound area. The sounds of the jungle disappeared following the gunshots, but have since returned, which is another good sign. My confidence is beginning to return.

I know the guardhouse is on the corner, so I pull off one of the LAWS and pull the pin, which arms the weapon. I nonchalantly walk out in front of the guardhouse, look directly at the camera, smile, wave, and press down on the trigger. Womp! The weapon kicks and sends the projectile into the side of the building. There is a large explosion and the guardhouse disappears in a cloud of dust and rubble.

I'm not sure what to expect next, so I quickly move through what is left of the gate into the dusty, darkened space of the inner compound. After a few seconds, the dust clears and I can make out the two copters and a faint view of the main house. Then the lights come on in and around the house. I can now see the entire bold outline of the estate.

I get down on one knee, pull the pin on the second LAW, aim and press down on the trigger. Thank goodness, the house is as large as it is. I really don't think I aimed that well, but there is no way I could miss. A large explosion erupts from the house as a ball of flames tops out at about 50 feet.

All of a sudden, I hear sounds behind me and as I turn with my M-16 at the ready, I recognize Colonel T along with Harley and Bos coming my way. I wave and yell out, "Take one of these LAWs and use it on the copters, I'm going in to use the last one on the house."

With adrenaline flowing and anger taking over, I take off toward the main house. I don't go any further than 50 yards, pull the pin, and just as I place the weapon on my shoulder, I hear an explosion and a large ball of flames light up the entire compound. I look back at the house, aim at an area still standing and press down on the trigger. I watch as the missile leaves a tracer-like path across the compound grounds before slamming into the house. The sound and explosion corresponds with the sound of a grenade exploding and the ensuing explosion and ball of fire coming from the copter pad.

I stand up and watch as the estate erupts into flames. There are no sounds coming from the house, and my only thought is, I warned you to leave me and my friends alone. I turn and go back to where Colonel T, Harley, and Bos have assembled. They are facing me and I yell, "Get down!" as I point my M-16 at them. They drop and I fire a burst of bullets over their heads at two guards who must have come from the guard position on the road leading into the compound. The guards drop. I get a thumbs up from the group.

"Let's get out of here," I yell. "This is going to be a very popular place before long."

We get on the 4x4s and head back to the airstrip. On our way back, Colonel T fills me in on what took place when he returned there earlier.

CHAPTER 68

Rick hears the gunfire and explosions. He watches the sky light up over the canopy of trees and then everything gets very quiet. The next sound he hears is the faint sounds of sirens in the distance. He says into his radio, "Come on guys, we need to get out of here right now."

"We're on our way Rick, get her fired up."

Rick jumps on board the plane and starts the engines. He turns the plane around and taxis back to the end of the runway where the large branch was located. He leaves the engines running, turns off the running lights, and waits as patiently as possible outside the plane with rifle in hand.

Five minutes later, we spot the one light from the guard shack at the airstrip. We turn off our lights and slowly approach the airstrip with weapons at the ready. We get off the 4x4s and quickly deploy in a defensive position as I say into my radio, "Rick, where's my damn airplane?"

Rick replies, "I'm up at the end where the limb was across the runway."

As we look in that direction, we see the outline of the plane. We also see faint lights coming up the path beside the airstrip. "Rick, you've got bogies coming up on your left, probably the roving guards. I guess they heard the ruckus and are heading back to the compound. We're on our way."

Rick whispers into the radio, "Thanks guys, I'll let them know we're here." He runs over to the side of the runway, puts his weapon on automatic, and sets up an ambush. When the guards get within range, he opens up and they never knew what hit them. He gets back onboard the plane, turns on the running lights, and says into the radio, "The guards are down. Get your asses up here, I hear sirens coming our way."

We hear the gunfire and we now see the running lights. We jump back on board our 4x4s and drive full speed up the tarmac toward the plane. We arrive just minutes later. The sirens are getting closer. We load everything on board and buckle up.

Rick hits the "GO" button and sends the AeroStar down the runway. We take off on a path that takes us over the compound and the estate. The house and both copters are burning. We see no signs of life anywhere. We do spot flashing lights coming up the main road and turning onto the road leading into the estate. We bank away from them, stay down on the deck, and head toward the Gulf of Mexico. Our journey is not over yet, not by a long shot. We still need to clear Colombian air space.

Not five minutes later, our worst nightmare takes place. We feel the windblast from two fighter jets whipping past us, one on each side. Rick is holding on tight to the controls but blurts out, "I hope somebody has a bright idea, or we're toast."

The fighters slow down and wait for us to catch up. We hear chatter on the radio, first in Spanish and then in English, "This is the Colombian Air Force. Take your plane back to the Bogotá Airport and land. If you resist, we will shoot you down."

Rick tips his wings to show he understands. He looks at me and I turn and look back at Colonel T., who gets out his phone and makes a call.

Rick begins a wide bank to take us back to Bogotá. Just seconds before we start our descent into the airport, we hear more chatter on the radio. "You have been cleared to proceed on your flight plan. Thank you for visiting our lovely country." The jets pull away and Rick banks the plane back toward the Gulf. We all breathe a sigh of relief. We are now alone in the moon lit sky.

I look back at Colonel T and he just shrugs his shoulders. "I know some people in high places who owed me one."

*****

Rick puts the plane on autopilot and we can all now relax and enjoy the flight back to Florida where we will stop and get fuel. After a couple of minutes, I say, "Thanks men. I appreciate the effort you all made tonight."

I am hoping tonight puts an end to my bickering with the Valdez cartel. The only responses I get are some grunts and snoring.

The ensuing trip back to Myrtle Beach is uneventful and very quiet. Once we arrive, I tell Rick to see if he can find someone to buy my plane and in the meantime, he can use it whenever he likes. I also tell him, as well as Harley and Bos, I will have checks for them tomorrow.

Once back at the house, Colonel T packs up and heads back to Ft. Bragg. I thank him for his help and tell him I owe him one. He tells me he has already made a note of that and put it on file.

I spend the rest of Tuesday sleeping and then go into the office early Wednesday morning.

I am pleasantly surprised when I get a call from Rick and he tells me I owe them nothing. He says they had a great time and to let them know if I ever need backup again.

CHAPTER 69

About 11:00 Wednesday morning, I call Detective Reynolds back in Lancaster. "Hey, what's the latest on Jake?"

"Nothing Mickke D, it's a cold case."

I am speechless for a few seconds. "Are you kidding me? That's it? Does everyone think he just disappeared into thin air?"

"That's about it. We have nothing to go on."

"That's bullshit, Detective, and you know it." I end the call and head back to Jim's office where I inform him I'm going to make a trip back to Lancaster in a couple of days and that he's in charge until I get back.

As I turn to leave his office, he asks, "How was the fishing trip with Colonel Townsend?"

I reply, "Very invigorating."

Jim just smiles. "I saw on the news that the Valdez cartel compound in Colombia was attacked Monday night, and all current members of the family are dead. The government has officially blamed another cartel for the attack."

He catches me by surprise, but I gain my composure quickly. "Wow. I hate to say it, but I suppose that's good news. Maybe that will end their attempts on my life as well as my friends'." As I'm leaving, I grin and say, "Thanks for the update."

"No problem. Hey, do you want me to watch Blue for you?"

"No, I think I'll see if Mark and Jannie will dog sit him for a few days. Blue likes their dog."

My next stop is at Jannie's desk where I ask, "Jannie, do you think you could take Blue for a couple of days? I'm going back to Lancaster, and I know Blue and Daisy get along and you guys have that huge fenced-in yard where they can run and play."

"Of course, we would be happy to dog sit Blue for you. Bring him over anytime."

On Thursday, I go over with everyone in the office what I need done while I'm away. I pack Thursday evening and drop Blue off at Mark and Jannie's. I leave early Friday morning for Ohio. I take everything with me that I had when I was up on Mt. Pleasant the last time, as well as two grenades left over from my trip to Colombia.

CHAPTER 70

When I arrive in town, I go directly to Shaw's but discover the hotel is closed for renovations. I end up going down the street to the new Mithoff Hotel on the corner of Main Street and Columbus Street, and get a suite on the top floor.

I notice the hotel is located across the street from the Paperback Exchange and since I forgot to bring some reading material with me, I'll stop by there tomorrow.

I go out to the Pink Cricket for a late pizza before turning in. I notice two women in a booth kind of staring at me, and then I remember them. They look like Terri Gandy and her golf pro daughter Samantha. I had met them at Dick's at the mall the last time I was in town because Terri was a witness I interviewed in a previous investigation.

As they get up to leave, I wave and they both walk over to my booth. Terri says, "Aren't you Mickke D from Myrtle Beach?"

"Yes, I am. I spoke with you out at the mall about the wreck on Allen Road."

"So whatever became of your investigation? Was it a black limo or a black SUV?" she asks.

"It looks like it was a black SUV that caused the accident. The owner of the vehicle is now deceased, so maybe justice was served."

"So why are you back in town, or did you ever leave?"

"No, I just got back in town this evening. I'm looking into the disappearance of a close friend of mine."

"Oh, is that the guy who's picture has been all over town and has been missing for a couple of weeks now?"

"Yeah, Jake Tracey. We went to high school together."

"Such a shame. We know Jake. He is our insurance agent. Hope you find out what happened to him."

"Nice seeing you guys." And, then looking directly at Samantha, I ask, "And how's your golf game, young lady? You and grandpa still cleaning clocks out at Valley View?"

"We do okay. Guess what? I got a golf scholarship to the University of South Carolina. I'm going to be in a Golf Management Program as well as playing on the golf team.

"Well, congratulations and best of luck. I hope to see you as a head golf pro somewhere someday."

"That's my goal," she says.

As they start to leave, Terri says in a rather provocative voice, "If you're ever out in the mall, stop by Dick's and say hello."

"I'll do that," I reply as I gaze at the ring on her finger. I guess I must really need some female companionship because even attractive married women are starting to look good to me.

Terri and Samantha turn and leave. However, there sitting in the booth they just occupied is Big Steve and his wife, Sharon. Steve motions for me to come over. Damn, I was hoping to get some investigative work done before he figured out I was back in town.

I pickup what's left of my pizza and saunter over to their booth. Steve says, "Sit," Sharon slides over. He starts in on me, "What the hell are you doing here? I thought I told you it was a cold case."

"So nice to see you guys as well." I give Sharon a side hug, which I can tell is not what she was expecting. "Well, if it's a cold case, why were those two ladies I was talking to telling me Jake's picture is all over town?"

"It's a cold case as far as the police are concerned. So again, why are you in town?"

"I just thought I would come back home for a small vacation. I needed a break from the action at the beach. I suppose you read about the terror threat to Charleston? Well, they were all killed in the Myrtle Beach area later on."

He leans back and crosses his arms over his chest. "Yeah, I read about it and I also saw you were involved in their demise. Well, whatever you do, don't shoot any innocent locals while you're here."

"So does that mean I can snoop around and you won't throw me in jail?" I ask.

"Take it any way you want, just don't shoot any locals."

The waitress comes over and they order. I add a beer and tell her to put it on his tab. Sharon sneaks a piece of my pizza as our conversation continues, "By the way, detective. Whatever happened to Von Spineback after he was acquitted?" I ask.

"Not sure. I think he is still in the Columbus area."

"And did they ever find the missing witnesses?"

"Not that I know of, but here's some news for you. Remember Detective Connehey, who you talked to in Reynoldsburg about your case? Well, he transferred down here. He's now on the force. Nice guy."

"Good, can't wait to meet him."

He grunts, "Maybe I should have him keep an eye on you while you're in town."

"I promise I'll be on my best behavior, detective."

Sharon laughs this time. "Yeah, right. What the hell do you have on this pizza?"

I smile. "Double anchovies."

With a grimace on her face, "Oh, my God, that's gross."

After they have finished their meal and when Sharon goes to the ladies room, Steve tells me what happened at the cave, including the smell and strange sounds.

"Yeah, I know. It was scary when I was there as well."

"So, level with me. Were you inside that cave?"

I hesitate. "Yes, for a very short time, and I couldn't wait to get out."

"What did you see?"

"There were tunnels leading every which way, and I sensed someone or something was in there with me."

Sharon returns and our conversation about the cave ends. As we all get up to leave, Steve says, "Stop by the station on Monday. I'll introduce you to Connehey."

"I'll be there. Nice to see you again, Sharon."

"You too, Mickke D. When are you leaving town?"

"Not sure, but we should get together again for dinner. This was fun."

Without replying, she just turns and walks out the door. For some reason, I think she still thinks I'm a bad influence on her husband. Steve follows her and raises his hand in a curt wave over his shoulder.

As I follow them out the door, I get that feeling on the back of my neck that I'm being watched or that something just isn't right. I brush it off. The Valdez family is dead, Jeffrey Barrons and Bob Linde are in custody in

Charlotte, and I, for once, can't think of anyone else who might want to kill me.

*****

Mickke D's feeling is not a fluke. There is another person in the restaurant that evening. He is sitting at the end of the bar and he came here to check on Detective Reynolds who just happens to be on his hit list. It's jackpot night, because another person on his list happens to be there as well, Mickke MacCandlish.

CHAPTER 71

On Saturday, I have breakfast at Root's. I do not see Samantha Gandy and her grandfather making bets for golf later on at Valley View. The group of men is there, however no fishermen show up to reel them in.

I return to my suite and later venture across the street and browse through the book selections at the Paperback Exchange. I find a few that sound interesting and take them back to my suite.

I drive through Rising Park in the afternoon but can't seem to get up the gumption to stop and take the walk up to the top of Mt. Pleasant. I plan to wait until I talk with Steve on Monday.

Sunday, I drive through Rising Park again. I actually sit on a bench and gaze at the path heading up the mountain, but I still can't make myself take the first step. I'm going to wait until Monday.

I guess everything that happened to me the last time I was up there affected me more than I thought.

CHAPTER 72

9:00 Monday morning, I walk into the police station and ask for Detective Reynolds. After checking my weapon at the front desk, I am ushered back to his office. As soon as he sees me, he gets on the phone. "Connehey and Turtle, I mean Barrish, will be right over to join us."

Before they arrive, I ask, "So why does Sharon seem so cool toward me? I haven't got you in any trouble for years."

"Yeah I know, but she has a memory like an elephant. Actually, I think she likes you in her own strange way."

"You could have fooled me," I reply.

Officer Barrish, who I recognize, and another man enter Steve's office. "Mickke D, this is Detective Ed Connehey, and I think you already know Officer Barrish."

I shake Barrish's hand and say, "Officer Barrish, thanks again for getting me off Mt. Pleasant. I don't remember much about it, but thanks."

"No problem, just doing my job."

The other man speaks up. "So you're Mickke D. I've heard so much about you. It's great to finally meet you." He takes a step forward and shakes my hand.

"Nice to meet you as well, Detective. What made you want to transfer down here?"

"Well, there wasn't much going on in Reynoldsburg, and this job became available. I thought it was time for a change. Have you seen Colonel Townsend lately?"

I stammer for a second and then reply, "As a matter of fact, he came down my way a couple of days ago and we went fishing."

"That's funny. I never knew he was a fisherman."

Thank goodness, Detective Reynolds changes the subject. "Okay, you two can catch up later. Let's talk about Jake. Turtle, could you please close the door and the blinds?" he says, as we all take a seat.

"First of all Mickke D, you're on your own on this one. The mayor and the powers that be have decided that it would be in the best interest of the city to not pursue trying to find Jake on Mt. Pleasant. They feel it is just too dangerous after the last incident. We cannot be involved, but we can bring you up to speed on what we saw and heard."

Connehey speaks up, "What about when we're not on duty?"

Reynolds replies, "What you do on your time off is up to you, but just remember what I said, the police can't be involved."

"Mickke D, if you need any help, just let me know." Connehey hands me his card.

"Thanks Ed, I appreciate that." I give him my card.

The three men go into detail about what they saw, what they heard, and what they smelled on that fateful day on Mt. Pleasant. They all admitted they were scared that day and all three seemed extremely remorseful about the fact that they did not go in and look for Jake, especially Steve.

At the end of their descriptions, I add what I saw while I was in the cave and then I ask, looking directly at Steve, "Do you remember anything like this ever happening on Mt. Pleasant before?"

"Not that I can remember," he replies. "There have been some small tremors over the years, but nothing like this. And it was only felt right where the cave was located."

I stand up and shake everyone's hand. "Thanks for the update, guys. I'm going to look around and see what I can find out. I'll keep you updated."

"Remember, Mickke D, don't shoot any civilians."

"Bad guys only, detective, bad guys only."

CHAPTER 73

Von Spineback is still pissed. He lost everything except his freedom. He was put on trial for being an accessory in the killing of a local newspaper reporter. After three of the prosecutor's star witnesses went missing, there was a mistrial and he was set free. He was forced to resign from Wilmont Gas & Oil and the majority of his assets were seized. He did not have a pot to piss in, or so everyone thought.

However, Von was smart. He had several offshore accounts that no one knew about. He started his own oil and gas consulting firm in Columbus and hired a small staff. One of the people he hired was James Mulhand. James replaced his former "solve all problems" guy, Stuart Peterson, who was killed on Mt. Pleasant by Mickke MacCandlish, a private investigator from Myrtle Beach.

James is a hired killer, aka "soldier of fortune" or "problem solver" who Von found online, and he came highly recommended. He was born in the U.K. and served in the army for six years. He left under questionable circumstances. He came to the United States ten years ago, got his green card, never renewed it, and got lost in the shuffle. He was excited when he spotted Mickke MacCandlish at the Pink Cricket, but not totally surprised. A friend in North Carolina who used to work with him back in the U.K. contacted him. She said she overheard a conversation, which made her think that he may be headed his way. Turns out, she was right.

Von had given him a list of four people to do away with, and the list is now down to two. The first two are deceased and their bodies will never be found. Those two, along with Ginny Ridlinger, Von's significant other at the time, were the only people who could tie Von to the murder of Sissy Adams, the newspaper reporter who died on Mt. Pleasant. Ginny died in Antigua at the hands of Von's twin brother, Dr. Jon Spineback, who also died in Antigua. That leaves Detective Steve Reynolds of the Lancaster Police Department and Mickke MacCandlish, aka Mickke D.

Killing any type of law enforcement officer is very risky and a little bit more difficult, but doable, and since he now knows Mickke D is close by, it will save him a trip to Myrtle Beach. He contacts Von and lets him know Mickke D is back in town.

Von Spineback blames Detective Reynolds and Mickke D for all of his past problems. If it weren't for them nosing around into the death of that newspaper reporter, he would be sitting pretty today.

He is happy to hear that Mickke D is back in town and he asks James to come to his office and discuss the matter. He wants to come up with a plan to kidnap Reynolds and Mickke D and make them suffer before they die.

James does not like the idea. He knows that the longer a person is kept alive, the more the chances are that they can cause problems, particularly if they are law enforcement. It's much easier to shoot them than to kidnap them.

CHAPTER 74

Following my meeting with Reynolds, Connehey and Barrish, I grab lunch and a beer at the Fairview Inn on Fair Avenue across from the Fairgrounds. After my second beer, I decide it's time to make another trip up Mt. Pleasant to have a look at the location of the earthquake.

I guess I'm still not in great shape, or it could have been my second beer, because I make two stops along the way to rest and catch my breath. As I near the crest, my mind wanders back to that night when I was shot and almost lost my life trying to catch a cold-blooded killer. The killer is dead, but it's hard to shake the events of that night.

I clear my head and take the same path I took that night, except I am walking instead of running for my life. There is a sign hanging from a chain supported by two metal posts at the point where the path begins, "Dangerous, Do Not Enter." I ignore the sign and start down the path. I notice several dead birds and dead squirrels along the path, which seems rather strange to me. The entire area almost has an evil feel to it.

As I near the location of the forked tree, I stop. The tree is gone and I see that everything on the other side of it, including the cave and the path, is gone as well. All I see is the rock-strewn side of Mt. Pleasant. It looks very natural but also foreboding in its own grotesque way.

I sit down along the path and close my eyes. I try to go back and remember everything I saw for the few minutes I was in the cave. I remember seeing several tunnels going off in different directions and an unpleasant smell. Of course, I was more concerned with what was happening outside the cave instead of what was going on inside the cave. However, after Reynolds and the others mentioned a clinking sort of metal-on metal noise, I vaguely remember that as well.

I get up and start to walk back toward the main trail, but suddenly I stop and turn around. If I remember several tunnels in the cave, what if that wasn't the only entrance? What if there is another opening somewhere?

Suddenly all is quiet, nature seems to be taking a break. A minute later, the sounds begin again, and so does the feeling that I am not alone up here. I instinctively touch my .45 to build my confidence and retreat back toward the crest of the mountain and the concrete steps.

As I get back to the steps at the crest of Mt. Pleasant, the evil feeling has disappeared and I have pretty much decided that I am going to go over to the other side of the mountain, off Fair Avenue, to look around.

I park on Lake Street just off Maple and walk back up the hill to Fair. I take the same path I took on the night I setup the ambush of Stuart Peterson. However, this time I take it slow and easy, looking for anything resembling another entrance to the cave complex. After about an hour, I end up right back at the crest of the mountain and none the wiser.

Either I'm wrong about the possibility of another entrance or I will need to spend a lot more time up here looking around. On my way back, I get that feeling that I am not alone, and it is not a good feeling. Something is going on here and I don't like it.

CHAPTER 75

Beverly Beery, Mickke D's on again, off again girlfriend, is back in Atlanta, trying to figure out if she wants to get out of her very dangerous line of work. She has really enjoyed the travel benefits and her salary, and she feels in her heart that the people she has eliminated deserved exactly what they got. They were all bad people and society is better off without them. However, the fact that she may never be able to have a meaningful relationship still bothers her.

Her worrying ceases when she gets a call from her boss, Liz Woodkark, aka GG, with a new assignment. Beverly tells her to send the info, and after looking it over, decides to accept the mission. She is thinking this may be her last rodeo.

CHAPTER 76

Ric Wertz and Terry Miller leave a bar in downtown Lancaster around 1:00 a.m. Tuesday morning and decide it would be fun to go up on Mt. Pleasant and fool around. Ric says they should not go through Rising Park because the police patrol it on a regular basis at night. He tells Terry that he knows of a back way off Fair Avenue. They park on Fair close to Madison and with a couple of beers and a blanket, they venture up to the old, rusty gate, which reveals a hidden path. They are trying not to laugh or talk too loud. Ten minutes into their adventure, Ric stops and says, "Shush, quiet. Did you hear that?"

Terry quickly responds, "Hear what? I didn't hear anything but I'm getting ate up by mosquitoes. Let me put that blanket around me."

Ric hands her the blanket and they continue on their way. Ten more minutes into their journey and deeper into the thick woods of the mountain, Ric stops again. "You didn't hear that? It was like someone banging pans together."

"Come on Ric, you're scaring me. Let's just turn around and go back. We can go to my place."

Without much thought, he responds, "Yeah, I think you're right, let's go."

The mosquitoes are the least of their worries. Screeches and screams fill the night on Mt. Pleasant, but they are not heard by anyone at this time of night and this deep into the woods. Ric and Terry waited too long to turn back. They never made it back to their car.

CHAPTER 77

Mid-morning Tuesday as I am thinking about looking around Mt. Pleasant, I get a call from big Steve. He tells me to come over to the station ASAP. I ask what's going on and he says he will fill me in when I get there.

I am confused. I don't think I have done anything wrong this time, at least not yet. Since the police station is only a few blocks away, I walk and when I arrive, he is waiting for me in the lobby. I check my weapon at the front desk and after he picks up a box of doughnuts, we proceed to his office. He takes two doughnuts from the box and takes the remainder over to the break room. He returns, closes the door, and asks, "Care for a doughnut?"

"No thanks." I reply.

He looks at the doughnuts, picks one up, puts it back down, and then begins. "There's a couple that has been missing since early this morning. Their car was found on Fair Avenue close to the mountain. The car belongs to Ric Wertz, the owner of Wertz's Auto Body Shop here in town, and we think the female is Terry Miller, an aspiring local artist, who has been doing painting classes around town. They've supposedly been a couple for about two months. They were last seen leaving a local bar around 1:00 a.m. this morning. No one has seen them since." After five seconds of silence, he continues, "Sort of reminds you of Jake, doesn't it?"

I get a sick feeling in my gut as I respond, "Yeah, it sure does."

CHAPTER 78

James decides it's time to make a head-on attack on Detective Reynolds. He has been following him for several weeks now, and the one thing he does every day at work is to have a dozen doughnuts delivered to the station at 9:30. James actually is in the lobby, wearing a disguise, while checking out where the cameras are located when the delivery guy brings the doughnuts. He watches as Reynolds goes into the first office, takes out two doughnuts and then walks down the hallway into what is probably the break room with the remainder.

James follows the delivery guy back to the doughnut shop and then he goes to a local consignment store and purchases some clothes that resemble the delivery man's uniform. He finds a jacket the same color, which will work. He also finds a ball cap the same color as the real delivery guy.

He purchases a dozen doughnuts the night before from the shop in the same box and same bag. He is wearing a wig, dark glasses, and a fake beard. He does not notice any cameras in the doughnut shop. Upon his return to his apartment, he injects a lethal poison into the doughnuts and returns them to the box.

He arrives at the police station at 9:15 the following morning, wearing his fake jacket and hat, along with his wig and dark glasses. He walks directly into the lobby area and stops dead in his tracks. There in the lobby is Detective Reynolds and Mickke D, who is checking his weapon at the front desk. He is now caught between a rock and a hard place. If he turns and retreats, someone may ask why is he leaving without delivering the doughnuts?

One cannot be shy in his line of work. He brazenly walks right up to Reynolds, keeping his back to the cameras and his ball cap pulled down over his face, and hands him the sack with the box of doughnuts inside. Reynolds takes the bag and says, “What happened to Jerry?”

He changes his voice tone and replies, “He’s a little bit under the weather today. I’m filling in.”

Reynolds reaches into his pocket to pay for the doughnuts, but the delivery person says, “It’s on us today, Detective. Enjoy.”

James turns and leaves the lobby. Outside he keeps his face turned away from the cameras. Just as he gets to his vehicle, which is parked on a side street with no cameras, the real delivery guy is pulling into the station. James smiles as he takes off the jacket and replaces it along with a new ballcap. He is thinking he would love to be there when the real guy shows up. He is pleased with himself. After today, he should have only one person left on his list, Mickke D. Of course, he could get lucky and Mickke D may have a doughnut.

That was fairly easy, he thinks. He could have shot both of them at the same time, but he was unarmed and in a police station. He figures the poison will do the job.

CHAPTER 79

After our short meeting, Steve walks me out to the lobby. As I'm retrieving my weapon, I hear him say, "Jerry, I thought you were sick?"

The delivery guy, with doughnuts in hand, gives him a funny look. "Not me, never felt better."

With a bewildered look on his face, Reynolds says, "That's funny, a guy from your company just delivered doughnuts fifteen minutes ago."

"That is funny. I'm the only delivery person. If I get sick, it's carry out only that day."

We both look at each other at the same time. Reynolds points at the delivery guy and says, "You. Stay here and don't move."

We both turn and run to the break room. The box of doughnuts is on the table and six are missing. I know Steve took two so that means four are missing. Steve runs back to the reception desk and gets on the intercom. "If you took a doughnut from the break room, do not eat it. I repeat, do not eat it! Lock the building down, now!"

We start down the hallway looking for the missing doughnuts. What we find are two officers and two secretaries coughing, gagging and turning blue. I look at Steve and yell, "Call 911! I'll get the box in the break room."

I get about halfway there when I am stopped by someone pointing a gun at my face. It's Detective Connehey. "Mickke D, what the hell are you doing? What's going on?"

"Follow me to the break room and put that damn gun away!" I reply.

"Right behind you," he responds, holstering his weapon.

We arrive at the break room and the six remaining doughnuts are still there. I close the lid, grab the box, and we head back to the lobby, stopping to place the two from big Steve's office back in the box. The paramedics have just arrived and are beginning to remove the victims. All seem to be alive and breathing.

I hand the box of doughnuts to Reynolds, who asks, "Did you get the two from my office?"

"Yes, I did," I answer.

He hands the box to Officer Barrish. "Go along and tell the doctors that whatever made them sick is probably in the doughnuts."

*****

After everything settles down and the building is searched and then reopened for business, Steve and I go back to his office. After several seconds of silence, he finally says, "How did that guy know who I was and that I was a detective? What the hell is going on here? Everything was nice and quiet, and then you get back in town and all hell breaks loose."

"I'm going to guess he has been watching you." Then I laugh and say, "And, how can you say that to someone who just saved your sorry ass?"

"I give up. And how did you do that?"

"Well, if I hadn't been here, you would have eaten both of those doughnuts and would be on your way to the hospital with the other victims. Be sure and let Sharon know that too."

"Good luck with that thought. She's going to blame you for the entire incident. The first thing she is going to ask is, 'Was Mickke D there?'"

We both laugh and then I ask, "So who in this town has it out for you and the police department?"

"I would guess that's a big list, but most of them are all talk. Why are you asking the questions? I'm the detective here. Why don't you get out of here and let me do my job."

"Yes sir, detective," I say and salute. Just as I am leaving, I turn and say, "Hey, what about our old friend Von Spineback? He could be blaming you and the police for his downfall. Did the delivery guy look like him at all?"

"I don't even remember what his face looked like. Hold on a minute." He gets on his phone and tells the officer at the front desk to make a copy of the tape from the cameras this morning and that he wants to see the tapes from the past week.

We wait patiently for the delivery of the tapes. They arrive on a thumb drive and we watch as it all takes place on his computer. The delivery guy knew exactly where the cameras were located and kept his back to them. His ball cap was pulled down over his face as well. There are no clear views of the man's face.

After reviewing the tapes from the past week, we notice the same man was in the lobby on Wednesday around 9:30 a.m. just as the doughnuts were delivered.

Reynolds and I both agree that the man caught on the cameras does not resemble Von Spineback, who is short and stocky, whereas this man is tall and rather thin.

"But that doesn't mean he didn't hire someone to do the job. He hired Stuart Peterson, didn't he?" I say, "Do you have an address for Mr. Spineback?"

"No, but even if I did, it's out of our jurisdiction."

"Yeah, but he's not out of my jurisdiction. I'd be happy to call on him and let him know we're keeping an eye on him."

Steve gets on his computer and runs Von Spineback's name. A consulting company comes up with the owner being a Mr. Von Spineback. Steve writes down the address and hands it to me. "This did not come from me and I would suggest you be very careful with this guy. Remember, you killed his right-hand man."

I give him a thumbs up as I'm leaving. "Keep your eyes open old buddy. Someone out there does not like you. Let me know if you find that missing couple. Also, lay off the doughnuts."

"That will not be a problem," he calls out.

*****

Minutes after Mickke D leaves police headquarters, Detective Reynolds receives a call from the hospital. All four victims are going to be fine. It seems as if they each had only taken one bite of the doughnut before Reynolds made the announcement on the intercom. They were a little bit stale and the poison gave the donuts a bitter taste. The doctor stated that if they had consumed the entire doughnut, they would all be dead. He concluded there was enough poison in each one to kill a horse.

He hangs up and says aloud. "Thanks, Mickke D, I owe you one."

CHAPTER 80

The local Central Ohio TV evening news stations have reporters doing interviews outside police headquarters and the following morning's local paper has large bold headlines: **Police Headquarters Poisoned.** The paper and the TV news both report that all of the victims are alive and well. They also both note that the police have no suspects at this time.

*****

Von Spineback watches the news and calls James. "What the hell happened, James? They're all still alive, and Reynolds wasn't even one of the victims."

"Mr. Spineback, all I can say is that they were all very lucky. Those doughnuts should have killed ten to twelve people."

"Well, they didn't. Now what are you going to do?"

"What do you think I'm going to do? I'll try again at another time and place," he angrily replies.

"Do you think they know it was you?" Von asks.

"No way, I had my back to the cameras and my hat pulled down. They have no clue it was me."

"Okay, keep me advised and do it right next time."

"Will do." James hangs up and begins thinking about his next attack.

Von Spineback is also thinking that he may have to get involved as well. He would love to catch Mickke D alone sometime. He touches the holstered weapon on the inside of his jacket and grins.

CHAPTER 81

After returning to my suite at the hotel, I look at the address Steve wrote down for me. The address looks familiar and then it dawns on me. That is the same address as Stuart Peterson's office in Reynoldsburg. Von must have taken over Stuart's old office or maybe he owned it and just let Stuart use it.

The following day, I make my trip to Reynoldsburg. I arrive in about 40 minutes and drive directly to Von's address. I sit in the parking lot trying to decide how I want to handle this. An idea comes to mind, and I call Detective Connehey back in Lancaster.

"Ed, I'm in Reynoldsburg and I need someone with the Reynoldsburg Police Department to come over here and park their cruiser in front of Von Spineback's office, so that maybe I won't get shot when I walk in the front door.

"Give me the address. Let me make a call and I'll get right back to you."

Five minutes later, he calls back. "Officer Tom Sampson will be there in about ten minutes. Fill him in and good luck."

I watch as Officer Sampson shows up fifteen minutes later at the appointed location. I notice a tall thin man walk in front of the cruiser and continue into the address I was given. He looks similar to the man I saw in the video at police headquarters, but there's not much I can do even if it is the same man.

I walk over to the cruiser where Officer Sampson is watching the front of the office. I knock on his window, startling him.

He opens the window and says, "What the hell are you doing, trying to give me a heart attack? What do you want?"

"Sorry, I'm Mickke D. Are you Officer Sampson?"

He calms down a little. "Damn, big Ed used to do that to me all the time. Yes, I am. What do you need me to do?"

"Well, for one thing, can you tell me why you refer to Ed as big Ed?"

He shakes his head. "Sorry, we are sworn to secrecy on that one. All I can tell you is it has to do with a photo."

"Thanks anyway."

"So what are you planning to do?" he asks.

There is a big difference between being brave and being stupid. After seeing who I think was the killer doughnut person, who tried to poison half of police headquarters in Lancaster, go into Von's office, I decide not to make a grand entrance. I notice the blinds in the front window are open. I figure I can get their attention just by letting them see me at the window. I feel much safer outside with Officer Sampson close by. I relay my plan to him.

"Officer Sampson, I am going over to that large window and try to get the attention of the people inside. I would like you to stand out here by your cruiser and observe, and be ready for the worst."

"No problem," he says as he exits his vehicle.

I cross quickly to the office window and peer inside. I see Von Spineback arguing with the tall, thin man and as they turn and Von points outside, probably at the

Reynoldsburg cruiser, they both notice me standing at the window. I wave, hold my fingers to my eyes, and then point both fingers back at them to show I'm watching them. I leave the window and walk back to stand beside Officer Sampson. We both watch as Von and his friend move to the window and peer out at us. After a few minutes, Officer Sampson gets back in his cruiser and I go back to my vehicle. We both leave the parking lot at the same time.

*****

Von Spineback is livid. "Do you believe that bastard?" he says. "We need to get rid of him, the sooner, the better. Follow him every chance you get and let me know if he goes somewhere where we can get to him."

"Will do, Mr. Spineback," James replies.

*****

Fifteen minutes later and just as James is leaving Von's office, another vehicle pulls into the parking lot. Mickke D and Officer Sampson are not the only ones watching Von's office today.

CHAPTER 82

Once I return to Lancaster, I call Steve and update him about what went on at Von's office. He tells me that he sent Officer Barrish and two other police officers to look around up on the Fair Avenue side of Mt. Pleasant and they found a blanket. The lab is checking it for any DNA.

Before I hang up, I ask, "Do you know how many missing persons have been reported here in Lancaster in the last year?"

"That's interesting that you asked that. We normally have very few reported missing persons, but within the last year we have had eighteen reported missing persons and not all of them have been from here."

"Have any of them been found?" I ask.

"Only two wives who took off for a couple of days just to piss off their husbands."

"So what happens to the ones who don't show up?" I ask.

"For an adult, we wait 48 hours and then we send the information to LEADS, a state and nationwide service for missing persons. The ones here in town are given to a detective who looks into it and they remain an open case until the missing person is found or identified."

"Are any of the missing persons cases drug-related?"

There's silence from Detective Reynolds and then he continues, "Oh, my God, we broke up a drug distribution ring six months ago that had been operating on and around Mt. Pleasant. Later, several of the suspects went missing."

"Did you ever find them?" I ask

"No. We just figured they skipped town."

"Sounds just like Jake and that couple."

*****

I spend the remainder of the day making phone calls and putting together a plan of action for what I figure will be an attack by the tall, thin man. I am really getting tired of people coming after me. I can still remember many quiet, peaceful days in Little River. Life seemed so much less complicated then, although not nearly as exciting. I guess I can't have the best of both worlds.

Tomorrow, I plan to go back to Mt. Pleasant and continue my search for another entrance to the cave. I am glad I brought everything with me that I did. I plan to use all of it.

CHAPTER 83

First thing the following morning, I call Detective Reynolds and tell him I will be looking around on Mt. Pleasant today, just in case a concerned citizen gives him a call that a strange man is wandering around on the mountain.

I leave the hotel around 10 a.m. and head over to Mt. Pleasant. I park on Fair Avenue and go through the old, rusty, metal gate big Steve described to me. I take the path where Steve said they found the blanket. He told me there are some flags stuck in the ground at the location.

I don't notice anyone following me, but I have the feeling someone is watching me. Once I get into the thicker part of the woods, I get off the path and wait. After fifteen minutes and nothing in sight, I move back to the path and continue my search. Five minutes later, I come upon the flags where they found the blanket.

The ground around the flags looks trampled down, I'm guessing from the police who found the blanket. I walk out about twenty feet from the flags and make a big left to right circle around the location. Then I reverse myself and make another circle, this time right to left. I don't see anything out of the ordinary.

Once I get back to the flags, I notice a big change. Nature has become still and I get a feeling of evil in the air. The back of my neck is bristling with nerves. I hear someone approaching and I am on full alert.

A woman dressed like a hiker appears on the path coming from the mountain. We exchange pleasantries as she passes by. She gazes at the flags and moves on as the sounds of the mountain return. As she disappears from view, my anxieties melt away.

Not allowing this strange feeling to deter me, I spend about another hour or so searching the area and come up with nothing. I finally surmise that if something did happen here, it happened at night after dark. I guess it's time for another adventure on Mt. Pleasant in the dead of night, something I am not looking forward to.

Once I get back to my vehicle, I call big Steve. "I am going up on the mountain tonight, except this time I'll be there right after dark and not in the middle of the night."

"Do you need any backup?"

"No, I'll be fine but thanks for offering. I'll call you if I get into trouble."

He laughs. "Mickke D, you always seem to be in trouble. At least that's what Sharon tells me."

"Very funny. Talk to you later."

*****

Several minutes later, a concerned citizen calls police headquarters to report a strange man in the area of Mt. Pleasant, just off Fair Avenue. The call is transferred to Detective Reynolds who informs the caller that the man is no problem and that he may be back in the area tonight, so don't be concerned.

James smiles to himself and thanks Detective Reynolds for the information. He then calls Von Spineback and tells him to come on down and to dress for a walk in the woods on Mt. Pleasant tonight.

Von is not much of a "nature" or "outdoors" type of person, so he puts on blue jeans, tennis shoes, and a white T-shirt. He puts his weapon in his waistband and leaves for Lancaster. He arrives about an hour later, just as the sun is setting over the mountain. He meets James at the fairgrounds entrance across from the mountain. James, dressed in camouflaged long-sleeve shirt and pants, boots and a floppy hat, looks at Von's attire and just shakes his head.

They take Von's car over to Fair Avenue and park at a location far enough away not to be seen, but close enough so that they can watch the metal gate. "Now what do we do?" Von asks.

"We wait, that's what we do. We wait until he shows up and goes into the woods and then we follow him."

"Whatever. Wake me up when he gets here."

CHAPTER 84

I arrive on Fair Avenue about an hour after dark and park as close to the metal gate as I can. I don't want anyone to see me enter the woods dressed in fatigues and combat gear, including my M-16. I spray myself heavily with insect repellant and start my journey. Again, I have the feeling I am not alone.

As I slowly make my way up the path into the deep woods, I can't decide if I'm looking for another cave entrance tonight or waiting for the tall, thin man to make his move. I get off the path at the same place I did earlier today. I find a tree to lean my back against and settle in for the night. I can see and hear anyone coming from either direction. I have a bottle of water and a pack of crackers. It is just another stakeout in the jungle, been there, done that, no problem. Five minutes later, I hear two clicks on my radio. I respond by clicking once. The tall, thin man has arrived.

*****

"Wake up Von, he just got here and is headed into the woods. Are you sure you want to go along? Maybe you should just wait here in the car until I get back."

After looking around at the darkness and thinking about the idea of going into the woods, Von replies, "That's a good idea. I'll wait here. Shoot the bastard once for me."

James whispers, "Okay, stay in the car. I won't be long." He leaves the vehicle and goes toward the metal gate with his revolver by his side. The hunt is on.

*****

Another vehicle arrives on Fair Avenue and the driver watches as a tall, thin man exits Von's car, and makes his way through the metal gate. The person is somewhat perplexed with what is going on, but the tall, thin man is not the target. The target is Von, and now he is alone in the car.

CHAPTER 85

Beverly Beery has been following Von Spineback for several days. Mickke D had mentioned Von when they met with GG, just outside of Atlanta for a possible job interview. He noted that Von had gotten away with murder by eliminating witnesses. GG must have looked into the situation and decided Von needed to go, hence Beverly's trip to Ohio. Then again, maybe GG was just trying to get Mickke D's attention. GG gave her the name and phone number of a person in Columbus where she could pick up a weapon and ammo.

GG had provided Beverly with Von's office and home address. She was watching him earlier this evening when he left his apartment with a gun in his waistband and headed south toward Lancaster. It is time to fulfill her contract.

Beverly had followed him to Lancaster where he meets up with another man who she has seen before at Von's office. They get into Von's car and leave. She follows. The two men park their vehicle on Fair Avenue. She is pretty far back, but she notices a car parked not far from a gate. A person gets out and goes through the gate, and heads into the woods. Not long after, the other man in Von's car leaves, with gun in hand and moves off into the woods. Von is now alone in the car.

Beverly is wearing black jeans, a black top, and black gloves. She takes a black scarf and wraps it around her head. The only part of her anatomy showing is her eyes. She gets out of her rented car and walks up to the car where Von is sitting with his eyes closed. He does not see her coming.

She knocks on the window, startling him, and he turns to see a gun with a silencer on it pointed at his head. His first thought is that the person holding a gun looks like a ninja warrior, and his second, and last, thought is why is this person pointing a gun at me?

Beverly says softly, "Liz sends her love," and pulls the trigger.

CHAPTER 86

If he stays on the path, he should be arriving within minutes. I have no idea what kind of a background this adversary has brought along with him, and I really don't care. He tried to poison most of the local police department just days ago and now is out here in the middle of the woods trying to kill me. He is my foe, my enemy. If I have to, I will eliminate him.

Suddenly I think to myself, Oh, my God, this is exactly what Beverly does, and I told her and GG I would not be comfortable doing such a thing.

Quickly, I convince myself this is different. This is personal. And besides, I may not have to kill him. He may be willing to surrender peacefully. Yeah, right.

I hear a sound, faint but definitely human, not animal.

*****

Beverly moves quickly back toward her vehicle, but just as she gets close, a man steps out of the shadows and forcefully says, "Do not move! Drop your weapon and get up against the car!"

Several things come to her mind. First, he has not identified himself. Second, from about ten feet away, he could miss. If he does, she will not.

"I'm Detective Connehey with the Lancaster Police Department. Get up against the vehicle, now!"

Well, so much for the idea of identification. Now her mind goes back to her training. If you are ever apprehended, do not resist. Call GG and she will find a way to get you out.

Connehey is getting frustrated. He has just watched this person shoot someone at point-blank range and they are not cooperating with his demands. "I will not say this again, drop your weapon and face the car."

She drops her weapon and moves up to the car. As he places her hands behind her back, she thinks about another part of her training. If you are apprehended by a single law enforcement person and you can escape without killing that person, do it.

As he begins to frisk her, Connehey says, "Oh, my God, you're a woman."

"No shit detective. You're good."

Before he can snap shut the handcuffs, she stomps her heel on his foot, and slams her elbow into his face. Before he can react, she has retrieved her weapon, and is pointing it at him.

She barks an order, "Now, let's reverse this whole situation. Against the car and spread your legs. Try something stupid and you'll be a tenor," as she moves her knee up towards his crotch.

Anticipating the upcoming pain, while trying to get over the existing pain in his foot and face, he replies, "No problem, lady. You're the boss."

She takes the handcuffs and puts one on his left hand, and hooks the other one to the luggage holder on the top of the vehicle. She takes the keys and throws them away, as well as his cell phone.

Detective Connehey can't believe how quick and how strong his female adversary is. He never knew what hit him. Now, he is handcuffed to the roof of someone's SUV and in a very uncomfortable position.

Before she leaves, she says to him, "Be sure and put in your report you were taken down by a girl and she let you live."

"Right, that will be the first thing in my report," he mutters as he watches her drive away in what looks like an airport rental car. He does not get a good look at the license plate.

Thank goodness, she missed the two-way radio in his back pocket. With his free hand, he extracts the radio and clicks it four times, pauses, and then clicks it two more times. This means, I'm in trouble and won't be there but I'm okay and not in a life and death situation.

*****

I hear the four clicks, the pause, and then two more clicks. Damn, now what do I do. I'm on my own with no backup.

In a situation like this, my instincts need to take over. I am listening for the sounds of nature all around me and the silence is unnatural. Now I need to listen for the sounds of humans.

Again, I hear a faint sound, maybe a step slowly taken, or an arm brushing against a tree limb or a bush. He is near. I catch a glimpse of him. He is prowling around the perimeter of my location, producing shadows of life-like hollow ghosts and goblins. He is so close I could reach out and touch him, but I am not sure if he brought Von along and if he did, where is he?

I command my heart rate to slow down and my breathing to slow down as well. I need to be motionless and quiet. He has no idea I am here. Suddenly all sounds cease. I get that feeling that something evil is near. Someone or something is very close and getting closer. I can see the tall, thin man maybe twenty feet away. Time for me to fish or cut bait.

I slouch down lower and call out, "You looking for me? Put down your weapon or I will drop you where you stand."

He looks my way, pulls up his weapon and fires. The bullet smacks into the tree just above my head. I point and pull the trigger of my M-16 twice. "Pop, pop." he drops to his knees and falls forward on the ground.

I slowly get up from my position and walk over to my fallen foe. I touch his neck. So much for the idea of taking him alive. I grab his weapon and stick it in my waistband. I get on my cell phone and call Steve. I tell him what happened and that Detective Connehey may be in trouble. I tell him where we are located. I jog back down the path to see what is up with Connehey. For some reason, I occasionally look back over my shoulder to see if anyone or anything is following me. The sounds of the night have not returned. I go through the rusty metal gate and hear Ed call out my name, "Mickke D, over here. Check the person in that car and see if they're alive."

I gaze into the vehicle he was referring to and I see Von Spineback slumped over in the front seat along with the shattered driver's side window. I find Connehey and notice he is handcuffed to the top of an SUV.

"What the hell happened to you? Who shot Von?" I ask.

"Well, I hate to say this, but some woman shot him. When I tried to arrest her, she got the drop on me and here I am."

I shake my head. "You're going to have a black eye tomorrow. What did she look like?"

"No idea. She was dressed in black pants, black shirt, black gloves, with a black scarf covering everything except her eyes. She was quick and strong. I never had a chance. I'm surprised she didn't shoot me as well."

The EMTs show up along with Steve. He gruffly asks, "What the hell is going on here? Connehey, what are you doing here and why are you handcuffed to that vehicle?"

I look his way and let Ed reply, "It's a long story Steve."

He gets out his handcuff keys and un-cuffs Connehey. "I can't wait to hear this one. Mickke D, where is the body?"

"Well, Von Spineback's body is up there in that car with the shattered window, and my dead body is about a quarter-mile up that path," I say, pointing at the rusty metal gate.

He looks perplexed. "I give up. Who killed Von Spineback? You, Connehey?"

He replies, "Not me. Some woman dressed like a Ninja Warrior shot him and when I tried to arrest her, she got the drop on me, and I guess you can figure out the rest."

With his arms folded across his chest, he says to Connehey, "And why were you here in the first place, detective?"

"Well, I was backing up Mickke D."

Reynolds looks at me. "I knew you had to be involved somehow. Why didn't you go to Pickerington High School, or Berne Union, or Amanda Clearcreek High School? That way, probably none of this would have ever happened."

"But detective, think about how dull your life would have been without me."

I pull the tall, thin man's weapon from my waistband. "Here's the weapon from your killer doughnut guy. He's about a quarter-mile up the path and literally right on the path. If you get to the flags where your people found the blanket, you've gone too far and probably stepped over him. You can thank me later."

Without replying, he turns and barks out a command to get a detail together to retrieve the body. He recruits two officers, along with himself, to escort the EMTs.

After they leave, I ask Ed, "Tell me more about the woman. Was she tall, what color hair, did she have long legs?"

"She was probably 5'10. She did have long legs. I have no idea what color hair, all I could see were her eyes. They were compassionless and cold. Why do you ask?"

"Oh, no particular reason. Just wanted to know some more about the woman who kicked your ass. Also, I promise not to call Colonel Townsend and give him the news."

"Very funny. The thing that still gets me is why didn't she shoot me? I am the only witness."

"Well, maybe it was a hit and you weren't part of the contract."

"You think she could have been a hired killer?"

"It's possible. Stranger things have happened." I reply.

Actually, it sounds a lot like a hit, and I think of Beverly. I told her and GG about Von when I met with them outside of Atlanta. I went into detail about how he hired the man who killed my friend's sister and then got rid of witnesses and got off scot-free. But, I did not ask them to get rid of him. I think I will keep these thoughts to myself for now.

Fifteen minutes later, my cell phone rings. It's Steve. "Mickke D, get your ass up here. We've searched high and low and there is no dead body here. Bring Connehey with you."

"What do you mean? He was dead. I shot him with an M-16. He had no pulse. He was dead! I even got his gun!"

He hangs up without replying. I look at Ed. "Let's go. Steve wants us up on the mountain. It seems as if my dead body got up and ran away."

As we approach the area where I had my encounter with the tall, thin man, I see flickering lights from flashlights and hear banter from the detail. I stop in front of the tree where I waited for my adversary. He is gone. The body is gone. I call out to big Steve, "Hey, back here."

Five minutes later, the detail shows up led by big Steve. "So where is the body?" he asks.

"Steve, he was right here on the path. I was sitting with my back against this tree. He fired his weapon at me and hit the tree above my head. I fired twice and he dropped. I felt for a pulse and there was none. He was dead."

I walk over to the tree, get my knife out of my pocket, and say to Connehey, "Ed, shine your light over here on this tree."

Connehey shines his light on the tree and I look closely for the lodged bullet, "Here it is." I dig out the lead projectile from the tree. I hand it to Steve.

He accepts the bullet and says, "That's nice. Can you dig the body out of the tree as well?"

I take my light and look closely at the area where I remember the body being located. "There, blood drops on the ground! They are moving away from the location." About twenty feet later, they disappear. I look at Steve with cold chills up and down my spine. "It's as if someone or something picked him up and carried him away."

All conversation ends and we all begin shining our flashlights around as nature's sounds disappear again.

Finally, Steve ends the silence. "All right, we are treating this as a crime scene." Looking at one of the officers, he says, "Tape this whole area off and get the crime scene boys up here right away. And don't anyone step in any of that blood trail."

He points to the two officers. "You guys stay here until the crime scene boys show up. The rest of you, head on back and stay on the trail. I don't want anyone else to disappear. Mickke D, Connehey, let's go."

I give him a stern look and pull him off to the side and whisper, "Are you sure you want to leave them up here alone?"

He looks at me and then he remembers the screeching sounds from the cave. He remarks to the two officers, "Okay, tape off the area and we'll all head back." The two officers look relieved.

All of us arrive back at Fair Avenue without any incidents. The EMTs take Von's body back to the morgue, and a towing company takes the car back to the impound lot. Steve tells me to meet him in his office at 9:00 in the morning.

I get in one last dig. "Should I bring doughnuts?" I get a, you're on thin ice look in return.

CHAPTER 87

The following morning, I arrive at police headquarters about 8:50. I check my weapon at the front desk and I am directed back to Detective Reynolds' office.

I knock on the doorjamb of the open door. Before I can say anything, Steve says, "You mention doughnuts and I'm going to deck you."

I laugh and reply, "No problem, I'm good."

Detective Connehey follows me in and Steve motions for him to close the door. Steve begins, "So Connehey, what were you doing over on Fair Avenue last night?"

"I got a call from Mickke D and he asked me to back him up. The plan was that if anyone followed him up the path, I was to call him on the radio and then follow at a discreet distance. I watched a man go through the gate and I notified Mickke D. Then as I was getting ready to follow, I see a person dressed all in black walk up to the car the man just got out of and shoot the person in the driver's seat. That's when I moved in, and I guess you know the rest."

I jump in. "I would like to know how he knew I was going to be there last night, unless he was following me around all day. If he was, I did not see him."

Steve gets a funny look on his face. "I may have the answer to that. I had a call forwarded to me yesterday afternoon about a strange man looking around on Mt. Pleasant. I told the guy he was okay, and that he probably would be back tonight as well."

I chide him, "Thanks detective. With friends like you, who needs enemies?"

He changes the subject. "And how did our killer know Von was going to be there?"

Connehey and I both shake our heads. I ask, "Any idea who the woman was?"

He replies, "We have no idea. She just seemed to disappear. And without a facial description, there's not much to go on."

Connehey says, "She was good, boss, I mean real good. Mickke D thinks it could have been a hit and that she was a hired killer."

"That right?" Steve asks, looking at me.

"Only because she didn't shoot Connehey as well. If it was a hit, he was not part of the contract, plus he was law enforcement."

Reynolds replies, "But why would anyone put a contract on Von?"

I reply, "I have no idea." Then it is my turn to change the subject. "So where do we go from here?"

"We wait for the forensic team to finish their thing up on the mountain today."

I leave Steve's office, pick up my weapon and head out the front door. I hear Ed call out, "Hey, Mickke D, wait up. So now what are you going to do?"

I think about the question. "I'm going back up on that damn mountain to find another entrance to that cave. I just know there has to be a second opening somewhere."

"If you need any help, just let me know. Sorry I wasn't more help last night."

"No problem, Ed. When is your next day off?"

"Tomorrow," he answers.

"Okay, meet me back on Fair Avenue tomorrow at ten in the morning. Fatigues and weapon."

"I'll be there."

After leaving police headquarters, I walk up Main Hill to the courthouse to try to find some topographic maps of Lancaster. I go to the Recorder's Office and I am met at the counter by a lovely young lady. "Well, hello there, my name is Rosemary. How may I help you?"

I allow my eyes to play over her well-formed body. Just watching those faultless lines frees my mind of all of my problems, if only for a moment. Finally, she asks again, "Ah, can I help you?"

I stop staring. "Well, I'm looking for some topographic maps of Lancaster. Do you have those here?"

She frowns. "No, I don't think we do, but I sure wish we did."

I give her my best flirting smile. "I wish you had them as well. So where should I go for those maps, Rosemary?"

"I think what you're looking for would be in the Engineer's Office." She yells out, "Hey, Gene, where can this guy find topogeographic maps or something like that?"

The man replies, "The Engineer's Office."

"See, I was right," she says. "If you don't find what you're looking for there, come back over here. I'll be happy to help you look around."

"Thank you, Rosemary, I may do just that."

As I move on to the Engineer's Office, I am thinking I may have to stop back by the Recorder's Office before I leave town.

Just before I enter the office, my phone rings. It's Steve. "Where are you?"

"I'm at the County Recorder's Office looking for maps."

He laughs. "Did you meet Rosemary?"

"Yes, I did," I reply.

"Hey, the DNA from the blanket matched both of the missing persons. Also, the guys returned from the mountain and said the blood spots were human but we have nothing to match them to."

"So what's next?"

"I'm going to send another search detail up on the mountain to look around."

"Great, but make sure it's during daylight and not tomorrow. Ed and I will be up there tomorrow looking around."

"Okay, no problem, we'll go up the next day. Let me know if you find anything tomorrow"

"Will do," I say.

I continue into the Engineer's Office and ask where I can find topographic maps of Lancaster. They point me to an area marked "Maps" and say if I need any help just holler. I look up the maps for the Mt. Pleasant area and take them over to a map table. I am looking for anything out of the ordinary, that might give me a clue as to where a second entrance to the cave might be. I find one very small anomaly, on the far back side of the mountain.

I take the map in question and ask the guy if I could get a copy of a particular section of the large map. He tells me no problem and charges me $1 for the copy.

As I leave the Engineer's Office, I ask myself if I should stop in the Recorders Office and say goodbye to Rosemary. Then I think to myself, Remember, Mickke D, women provide the greatest of pleasures and the worst of problems.

I slow down as I pass the office but decide to heed my own warning and keep going. I need to stay focused on the mountain so I can find out what happened to Jake.

CHAPTER 88

Once I get back to my hotel suite, I start getting things ready for tomorrow morning. Not long into the process, I decide I have to call Beverly and see where she was last night. I know she won't admit it, but I just want her to know that I know what she did.

She answers after four rings. "What do you want?" Her voice is cold and toneless.

I get right to the point. "Were you in Lancaster, Ohio, last night?"

I can tell the question catches her off guard, but she quickly recovers. Her tone does not change. "Of course not. I don't even know where Lancaster, Ohio, is. Why do you ask?"

"Because I'm in Lancaster and last night someone shot and killed Von Spineback. Remember, I told you and GG about him when I met with you ladies outside of Atlanta?"

She hesitates and then answers, "Sorry, not me. I'm in Atlanta. Been there since I left Myrtle Beach. Why are you in Lancaster? Were you going to eliminate the guy and someone beat you to it?"

"No, I am here trying to find out what happened to a friend of mine who disappeared."

"Anything else, Mickke D?"

"Yeah. Thanks for not shooting Detective Connehey."

She abruptly hangs up.

CHAPTER 89

I awake the following morning to a beautiful sunrise and a forecast for a very awesome early fall day in Ohio. Looks like a great day for a leisurely walk in the woods. I place two bottles of water, some protein bars, duct tape, two extra ammo clips for my .45, two two-way radios, my maglite, the copy of the map I made in the Engineers Office, an ammo belt, two flares and two grenades, in my backpack. The grenades were left over from my 'fishing trip' to Colombia. Colonel T never asked for them back and I never offered to give them back. I know deep down that he knows I still have them.

After breakfast at Root's, I change into fatigues and I arrive on Fair Avenue about 9:50. Detective Connehey pulls in right behind me. I ask if he's ready to go. He gives me a thumbs up. We walk through the rusty metal gate and once on the other side and out of sight of any civilians, I stop and open my backpack. I hand him one of the two-way radios. I strap on my ammo belt and take the two grenades from my backpack. I attach them to my belt.

"Damn, Mickke D, I didn't know we were going to war. Where in the world did you get those?"

"You really don't want to know. Hopefully we won't need them." I pull my shirt down to cover the grenades, in case there are any civilians in the area. "Do you have your badge with you in case we run into any civilians along the way?"

"Yes sir, back pocket. So do you have a plan? Are we just winging it?" he asks.

"Probably a little of both." I retrieve the map from my backpack and hand it to him. "I would like to look at this area of the mountain." I look him in the eyes and ask, "So what do you think was in that cave?"

"I don't know, but it scared the hell out of me. I'm glad Steve decided not to go in that day."

"Tell me about it. I was in there for a very short time and it sure got my attention. But here's the thing. I saw several tunnels running in different directions so that's why I think there has to be another entrance somewhere. Whatever was in there had to be able to get in and out, and the vines on the rock wall were not disturbed before I cut some of them and went inside."

"Well, it looks to me like we are about here," he says, pointing to the map.

"Yeah, I think you're right. Let's just take our time and see what we can find. I've got some protein bars and water in my backpack. Let's start where I shot the guy who disappeared and then move up to where they found the blanket. Are you ready?"

"Let's do it," He says as we move out.

We keep any conversation to just above a whisper as we head up the path toward the location where I had my encounter with the tall, thin man. Once we arrive, we look around and nothing looks disturbed or matted down. I find the blood trail and again, it just disappears. I say, "It doesn't make any sense. If he was dragged, there would be a trail. He had to have been carried."

Ed moves out about ten yards. "Oh my God! Look at this Mickke D!"

I walk over to where he is standing and gaze down at the ground. There in some loose soil is a single footprint. "Holy shit. What the hell is that?"

"I don't know, but I've never seen anything like that before," he replies.

I get out my phone and take several pictures, and Ed does the same with his phone. "Is anyone going to believe this?" he asks.

"I don't know. I'm not sure I believe it."

CHAPTER 90

After she hangs up from her call to Mickke D, Beverly thinks back to the shooting in Lancaster. She believes she followed protocol by allowing the detective to live.

Afterward, she drove her rental car to a motel on Route 33. A black Suburban was waiting to ferry her to the Lancaster Municipal Airport where a Learjet was waiting to transport her back to Atlanta.

While still going over what took place, her phone rings. It's Liz, "So I guess things didn't go smoothly the other night. I saw where the Lancaster Police put out a BOLO on a woman suspected of killing a man in Lancaster. Not much of a description and no leads so far."

"You're right. The operation went fine. As I was leaving the scene, I was stopped by a Lancaster detective who just happened to be there, probably on a stakeout. I got the drop on him, handcuffed him to an SUV, and left. In the struggle, he figured out I was a woman. Did I do anything wrong?"

"Of course not. We never want to harm a fellow law enforcement officer if it can be helped. So no one else saw you that night?"

"Not that I know of," She replies.

"Great, Beverly. So is everything else okay with you? Have you seen Mickke D lately?"

She answers truthfully. "No, I have not seen him, and I don't plan on seeing him. He's history as far as I'm concerned."

"Well, good for you."

Liz is starting to be concerned about Beverly. She does not believe Beverly is over Mickke D and she worries that since he knows a little bit about their operation, the whole thing could become a big problem. She also believes that it may not be long before she receives Beverly's resignation. She has a new girl starting soon and she wanted to send her to Beverly for some training, but now she's not so sure.

CHAPTER 91

The footprint has to be eighteen inches long. It has six toes and it is a skeleton print, nothing but bones.

We are both looking at the footprint when we hear the sounds. I raise my fist and point up the path toward the area where the police found the blanket. We both move behind trees and our fatigues blend in perfectly with our surroundings. Only a trained military person would spot us. We remain perfectly still as we hear the sounds of someone talking and walking toward us.

I cautiously peer around the edge of the tree and spot the source. It's an old man dressed in tattered jeans, an old sport coat or suit coat, a beat-up Ohio State ball cap, and well-used tennis shoes. He is talking to himself. I glance at Ed, point him down toward the path where we just came from, and motion that I'm going in from this direction.

Ed silently moves off and I move in, showing myself just as the old man gets to within fifty feet of me. I call out, "Hey old timer, how are you doing?"

He stops abruptly and looks my way. "Well, I guess I'm okay. What are you doing out here? Are you going to rob me? I don't have any money. Are you part of the devil's clan?" His voice sounds much younger than his physical appearance. His face turns crimson as he takes a step backward as Ed appears on the path in front of him.

I answer, "No, we are not here to harm you or rob you. We are with the Lancaster Police and we're just out here looking around for some clues in a kidnapping."

He takes another step backward. "Are you going to arrest me? The devil is the one who did it."

"No, we are not going to arrest you." I reach in my backpack and say, "Would you like a protein bar and a bottle of water?"

"Oh yes, that would be wonderful." He comes forward and grabs the bar and water but in doing so, he steps on the loose soil where the footprint was located. I start to yell at him, but I decide I don't want to scare him off. Besides that, Ed and I both have photos. I touch my pocket where my phone is and it feels warm and then suddenly cold.

I take a deep breath and continue, "Do you mind if I ask you some questions? What is your name?"

He looks at me with disdain in his eyes. "People call me Willie. Will you arrest me if I don't answer your questions?"

I try to gain his confidence. "Of course not, Willie. We were just hoping you could help us out with this kidnapping case."

He looks at Ed and then at me. I figure he's thinking there's no way he can outrun both of us. He finally answers, "Sure, what do you want to know?"

"So, Willie, where do you live? Have you seen any strange people or animals out here in the woods?"

"I live a lot of different places, and I haven't seen anything except the devil."

"Does the devil live out here in the woods?"

All congeniality fades from his face. "Didn't you hear me? Of course he does."

"Where does he live? Can you show us?" I ask.

He takes another step backward. "I can tell you where he lives, but I am not going with you or anywhere close to that place. When he gets hungry, he comes out at night and people disappear."

"No problem, Willie, just tell us where he lives."

He points up in the woods. "Go up that way about half a mile and be real quiet. He does not like loud noise."

I look at Ed and he nods his head. I nod back, reach in my pocket and say to Willie, "Thanks Willie, here's a twenty. Go buy yourself a good meal."

He grabs the twenty and takes off down the path, moving rather quickly. Ed says, "He pointed in the direction you wanted to go. What do you think?"

"I think we should head that way and be very quiet. We don't want to piss off the devil."

"Should we call for backup?"

"Let's wait to see if we find something. If we call Steve and he brings a squad of officers out here and there's nothing here, we'll both be in big doo-doo."

"Yeah, you're right about that."

We take about ten steps and I abruptly stop, turn around and say to Ed, "Did you notice how large Willie's feet were? And was it just me, or did his voice sound like a much younger person?"

"They were pretty big weren't they? They almost looked like clown shoes. And yes, his voice did not match his looks. He was a strange dude."

I turn and Ed follows me back to the place where we found the footprint and where Willie stepped on it while coming for the protein bar and water. I say, "That's interesting; his tennis shoe print is the same size as the footprint."

Putting his foot beside the imprint of Willie's shoe, Ed remarks, "Has to be a fifteen or sixteen, don't you think? That's pretty large for a guy no bigger than Willie."

"Yes, it is strange. He was strange. Oh well, let's go wake up the devil."

We set off in the direction Willie pointed. The deeper in the woods we get, the denser the trees become and the slower we travel. Thirty minutes later, we stop for a break and Ed checks the topo map. He half-whispers and points, "The area you circled on the map has to be right over that rise."

I pull my .45 and Ed pulls his .9 mm as we slowly proceed. We get to the top of the rise, crouch, and gaze at the area in front of us. The trees thin out about fifty yards straight ahead and a small hill is visible. It almost looks like an old Indian mound. The face of the mound is covered by the same type of vines that covered the cave entrance on Mt. Pleasant.

Ed whispers, "Now do we call for backup?"

The demons inside my belly are beginning to move around, and I am tempted to say yes. "Not yet, we still haven't found anything."

He looks at me and whispers, "You're not going to do anything stupid like that Claymore Mine thing back in Colombia, are you?"

"Of course not. I just think we need more evidence before calling in the troops."

"So what is your plan, or do I really want to know?" he asks.

"Okay, here's the plan. I'm going up to that mound to see what's there, and you are going to stay here and cover me. Use the radio sparingly; remember, the devil does not like noise. If everything is okay, I'll motion for you to come on up."

"Roger that. Be careful."

With my weapon at the ready, I slowly venture out from the confines of the heavily wooded area into an area with sparse trees and waist-high brush. It doesn't take me long to traverse the area and arrive at the vine-covered mound. I pull on the vines and they give way to reveal what looks like a cave entrance. I back away to the side of the mound and motion for Ed to come on up.

He moves up and crouches beside me. "Is it an entrance?" he whispers.

"Yes, I'm pretty sure it is. I had no problem pulling the vines apart. It's coal black inside and smells just like the entrance over on Mt. Pleasant."

"My God, the cave has to be three-quarters of a mile long. So now what?"

"What was your rank in the service?" I ask.

"E-6. Why do you want to know?"

"Well, I was a 1st Lieutenant so I outrank you. So you're going in to look around."

"Bullshit. That was your friend who went missing. I never knew him. Let's call for backup."

I chuckle, "Just kidding, Ed. I'm going in and you're going to stay here and monitor the radio. If things go bad, then you can call in the troops."

I move over to the vine covered entrance, and just as I begin to cut the vines apart and prepare to go inside, we both hear a blood-curdling screech from the cave. I back off and return to where Ed is crouched much lower than before. "Damn, what the hell was that?" I ask.

He whispers, "That was the same sound we heard just before and during the earthquake the other day."

I look at Ed. "Okay, now you can call for backup. I'm still going in. Keep your radio close but don't call me, I'll call you. Direct the troops to our location. Also, if they come in before I come out, be sure and let them know I'm in there. I don't want to get killed by friendly fire."

Ed nods his head and gets on his cell phone as I creep forward.

I have always believed that fear gives you greater strength than anger. Well, if that's the case, I should be real strong, because I'm scared to death. If you have ever been in a cave with no light, then you've been in total darkness. You literally can't see your hand in front of your face.

I move to the entrance and slowly finish cutting the vines. I flip on my maglite and check the time. 11:10 a.m. The same screeching wail resonates through the darkness. It's now mind over matter. I ignore the sound and move inside. The vines close behind me. I move my maglite around and see two tunnels going off from the main entrance. Then I notice a shadow dart down the right-hand tunnel. I decide it would behoove me to take the left-hand tunnel. With my .45 at my side and the maglite leading the way, I venture forward very slowly, stopping occasionally to listen for strange sounds. I continue seeing shadows but when I shine my maglite, they are gone.

The floor of the tunnel is probably ten feet wide and the ceiling is about eight or nine feet high. The floor, walls, and ceiling are all a charcoal grey/black color. The tunnel has a burnt smell to it as well as a dead smell. It's as if the sandstone had caught on fire and this was the end result.

I continue to navigate my way down the tunnel. I can tell I've been going slightly downhill since I started my journey. I look at my watch again and it is 11:40. I figure it will take Steve and his men at least an hour to get up here, maybe longer. I think about turning around and heading back, but again it's mind over matter.

I see a bend in the tunnel up ahead, and I gingerly approach with caution. I begin to notice a faint greenish hue coming from around the curve in the tunnel. As I turn the corner, I shine my maglite and see what looks like a large cavern, almost a room right in front of me. I have not heard any strange sounds or seen any shadows lately, so I slowly continue moving toward the room. I stop at the end of the tunnel and lean my back against the tunnel wall. I take a deep breath and decide to call Ed.

Just as I hit the switch on my radio, my maglite flickers and goes off. "Damn," I whisper as my heart rate increases and my fear level explodes. I quickly tap it a few times. It comes on full power again. I take a deep breath and whisper, "Ed, are you there?"

He replies, "Yes, how are things in there? Are you okay?"

Whispering again, I answer, "Yes, I've stumbled upon a large room down here and I'm getting ready to check it out. Are the troops on their way?"

"Yes, they are. ETA at about 12:30. Unless you want me to stay, I'm heading back down to the main path to meet them and lead them up here. I figured it might be quicker that way."

I hesitate. "Okay, but don't mess around, get your ass back up here ASAP. This is one scary place. Call me when you return."

"Roger that."

I open a bottle of water from my backpack and take a long drink. I move slowly into the room. It is probably 100' x 100' with a curved ceiling, probably twenty feet high. Again, all the walls are that same dark charcoal black/grey color and the smell is getting stronger. I see bones lying on the floor in piles.

I walk over to the nearest pile, place my weapon in my waistband, and pick one up. It seems to be human. I see what looks like jewelry beside the pile, as well as a small rusty metal box. I pick it all up. The jewelry consists of several rings and necklaces. I get a sick feeling in my stomach as I recognize one of the rings as one that Jake had worn on his pinky finger. I place everything in my backpack.

I go to the next pile and notice some of the bones are a bright, almost lucent color. I pick one of those up and it appears to be very light and almost metallic. I secure a second one and touch them together. It's a metal on metal sound.

I'm paying too much attention to the bones and not enough to my surroundings. I suddenly get the feeling I am not alone. I jump as another screech fills the room. I drop the bones and secure my weapon. I move my light around, look up, and there about thirty feet in front of me is a figure and it looks to be human.

Now I know this is impossible and most likely an illusion. I look at his feet and they are huge. My mind goes directly back to Willie for some reason. He speaks and the voice sounds just like Willie's voice. "Why are you here? You need to leave."

The hairs on the back of my neck are standing straight up. So now, how do you answer an illusion? I come up with, "No problem, I'm just passing by and on my way out. Sorry if I disturbed you."

I have been in some tight situations before, but I think this one takes the cake. I move backward toward the tunnel and press my back against the wall. I sneak a peek around the corner and that's when I see it. The human figure is no longer there, but something else has taken its place.

CHAPTER 92

"Oh, my God! What the hell is that?" I say aloud. It looks like some sort of a creature or a skeleton, but whatever it is, it is not human. The creature has to be seven to eight feet tall with jade green eyes that are radiating a green hue throughout the room. As the eyes get brighter, the room begins to glow.

I move away from the wall and point my weapon at the creature, but I don't fire. I'm aiming at a skeleton. What are the odds of me hitting it? Even if I do, how do you kill something not human? I point my maglite at the skull, and again that bone-chilling wail comes out of its mouth. The bright light seems to really piss the thing off.

I think about the pile of bones and Willie. Oh, my God. What if there's more than just one of these creatures? What if there is a whole tribe of them in this cave? Who are they? What do they want? Is this one the head honcho? I place my weapon back in my waistband and take off a grenade.

I pull the pin and toss the grenade. The creature, or whatever it is, looks down and then back up at me with green eyes blazing, as I duck behind the tunnel wall and cover my ears.

The grenade explodes and sends shrapnel everywhere as well as dust and debris billowing through the tunnel. I hear bones' clanging off the walls, as a powdery fog fills the room. As the fog slowly dissipates, I shine my maglite around the tunnel and the room. There are no sounds, and I don't see any creatures.

I quickly decide it's time to leave. My body hurts. I think I've been hit by shrapnel, but before heading out, I break a flare and toss it into the room. I have a funny feeling there are more of the creatures around. Suddenly flames erupt in the room and high-pitched screams and screeching fill the room and tunnel. I turn and start to run toward the vine-covered entrance. I hear screeching not far behind me, so I stop, grab the other flare, break it, and toss it down the tunnel. Again, fire erupts and smoke billows down the tunnel. More screams fill the air.

I begin running again. Finally, I can see the entrance in front of me and I don't even think about slowing down. I plunge through the vines and I'm temporarily blinded by the bright sunlight. I hit the ground and roll over, grab the last grenade from my ammo belt and pull the pin. I toss it through the vines into the cave. I hug the ground and cover my head as the grenade explodes. I sit up as the dust clears. The entrance is gone.

Just then, the ground begins to shake and I scramble on my hands and knees away from the mound. As the shaking subsides, I look back and the entire mound is gone.

CHAPTER 93

I wake up and discover I am sitting against a tree on the edge of the clearing. I look at my watch and it's 12:45. I feel like a truck ran over me. I look myself over and I notice several parts of my body have blood on them. I faintly hear sounds approaching and I actually see Ed, Steve, and the troops before I hear them. My ears are still ringing.

They come out of the deep woods and rush up to me. Ed says, "Damn, Mickke D, what happened to you and what was that explosion we heard?"

I just stare at him and don't answer. Steve asks, "Are you all right? You look terrible."

I just nod my head. Again, I don't answer.

Steve and Ed look around for a short while. The vine-covered mound is gone. There is nothing left to show anyone it had ever been there. Ed places a couple of flags in the ground where he remembers the mound once stood. Then, after I get my legs back under me, we head back. The EMTs are waiting for us on Fair Avenue and they attend to my wounds. Steve says he wants to see Ed and me tomorrow morning, first thing.

I return to my suite at the hotel and try to make sense out of everything that happened today. It's mainly a blur in my mind and at times I'm not really sure it happened at all.

I have no idea what those creatures were, but they had the ability to transform themselves into humans. Maybe that is the only way they can converse with us. As far as to how they got here and how long they have been here, I have no idea. I just hope the cave is sealed and the fire destroyed all of them, except for maybe Willie.

I check my backpack and the rings, necklaces, and metal box are still there. I place the box on a table; get out my penknife and pry open the rusty lid. Inside, I find what looks like a diary with the initials M.M. on the cover. Oh, my God, there have been stories for years that she was in Lancaster and spent time on Mt. Pleasant., but how would her diary end up in the cave. I open it, read a few pages, but decide I'm too tired. I'll let Steve have the honors.

I go to bed early, but I don't get much sleep. Nightmares about skeleton creatures and black walls closing in on me keep waking me up. I skip breakfast in the morning, except for some orange juice. I get to police headquarters around 8:30 and start to check my weapon, only to realize I forgot to bring it with me. The officer at the front desk ushers me back to Steve's office. The mayor and police chief are there. Ed joins us right after I arrive.

I go over everything that happened yesterday in vivid detail including our encounter with Willie and the minor earthquake. No one present interrupts me along the way. After I finish, the mayor looks at me and says, "Do you really expect me or anyone else to believe that story? Do you want to panic the entire city of Lancaster? Do you have any proof? Do you have any pictures or anything else to back up your story?"

The police chief looks at Ed and interjects. "Detective Connehey, did you see any of this?"

Ed looks at me and answers, "No, I didn't see anything but I heard the screams and screeching sounds coming from the entrance of the cave."

Steve says, "We all heard those same sounds up on Mt. Pleasant during the earthquake."

The mayor responds, "Probably just a misplaced owl or a bobcat, or both."

I am very close to being totally pissed off, but instead of going off on them, I grab my phone and say, "I do have a picture of the footprint Ed and I found."

I hit photos on my phone and click on the picture. "Well, I'll be damned," I whisper. "Ed, check your photo of the footprint."

Ed gets his phone, finds the picture and looks at me. "The footprint is gone. All I have is a picture of the tennis shoe print."

I reply, "Yeah, me too. What the hell is going on here?"

Steve butts in. "So neither one of you have any solid proof of what went on up there yesterday?"

"Steve, we both saw the footprint." Ed says.

"I believe both of you, but without cold, hard proof I am not going to put any of this out to the public."

The mayor says, "I concur."

"We can always go back up there and excavate the site and find the cave." I say.

"That's not going to happen, gentlemen. Let's just leave well enough alone," the mayor remarks.

I have been saving the best for last. "Okay, have a look at this," I say as I place my backpack on the table. "I found these in the cave." I place the rings, necklaces, and rusty metal box on the table. I point to one of the rings and say to Steve, "Jake was wearing this ring the last time I saw him. Go ahead, open the metal box."

He opens the box and takes out the diary. He smiles, "People here in town have talked about her being up on Mt. Pleasant for years. Hell, anyone could have put this in the cave." He pauses as he pushes the diary toward the mayor. "But we will have it analyzed by an expert. It still doesn't prove anything."

"What about the rings and necklaces?" I ask.

"We'll check those out as well," he replies.

*****

As I leave police headquarters, I'm frustrated and pissed off. I am completely spent. I just know nothing is going to come out of any of what I saw or found on Mt. Pleasant. I'm tired and I hurt. I guess I'll just pack up and head back to the beach. I need a break from this crazy summer.

*****

It's been three weeks since my return to Little River. My body has finally regenerated itself and my demons are slowly disappearing. I am feeling less threatened because the Valdez cartel is gone. Maybe, I can stop looking over my shoulder. On the down side, I still have nightmares about Mt. Pleasant and the cave creatures.

Then, I receive a text from Detective Reynolds. It reads: I have good news and bad news. Good: We have determined that the ring did belong to Jake and that some of the other jewelry did belong to several of the other missing persons. Bad: The diary has disappeared and The State

Geological Academy has determined that Mt. Pleasant is too unstable to have any further excavation done. Case closed.

The End

EXCERPT FROM "MURDER ON THE FRONT NINE"

I sluggishly and slowly pull myself out of bed around 7:00 a.m. It's Saturday morning and I heard my overnight guest leave about 6:30. She told me last night she had to be at work by 7:00 at some resort on the ocean. She was a cute, well put together young woman with freckles, I'm guessing in her mid-twenties. I must have really made a big impression on her because she did not even say good-bye. She did leave me note which read, Mickke D, been fun but my boyfriend will be back in town tomorrow. See ya, "pops."

She never mentioned she had a boyfriend and what is this "pops" bit? Oh well, there are quite a few available women in Myrtle Beach. Of course, sometimes I feel as if I've been married to most of them.

I walk into my bathroom and with blurry eyes gaze soulfully into the mirror. Staring back at me is a forty-five year old single male about 6'1" 190 pounds with sandy blond hair. He looks to be in pretty good shape when he pulls his stomach in and throws his shoulders back. Maybe not the buff, ex-Green Beret he was after mustering out of the army fifteen years ago, but not a "pops."

EXCERPT FROM "COUGARS AT THE BEACH"

The sun propels its first shafts of sunlight, brightening the sky from violet, to salmon, to blue as early morning dawns in the mountains of Colorado. A deafening silence claims the cold, thin, clean air.

A female cougar is stalking a snowshoe rabbit. She has been on the rabbit's trail since the sky turned from dark to pale. She finally spots her prey about 100 yards away. She has been using her keen sense of smell up to this point and now she finally has her first meal in three days in sight. All of her senses go viral. Her taunt muscular body is ready to pounce, her pupils are wide open and her ears are at attention. She flexes her razor sharp claws in the freshly fallen snow. She moves with quiet stealth to get nearer to her prey. She gets to within fifty yards of the rabbit when he turns and sees her crouching in the snow. He cowers with fear and anticipation. She freezes; the wind is motionless and there is not a hair moving on her beautiful coat of winter fur.

EXCERPT FROM "DEATH ON MT. PLEASANT"

Once she reaches the beginning of the trail, she slows her pace and gazes at the reasonably short, steep climb to the top of Mt. Pleasant awaiting her. She realizes, at age 40, this will not be as easy as it was in her teenage years. Motivated by the information she hopes to glean concerning her story, she begins the uphill climb. She starts her climb slowly but it isn't long before she is breathing hard, and she can feel her heart pounding in her chest and ears. She seriously thinks about turning around and going home. She closes her eyes and forces herself to focus on what she stands to gain once she reaches the top.

After resting for five minutes, she continues her journey. Once she has gone about three-quarters of the way up and after a sharp right-hand turn, she pauses to rest again, during which she tries to build up her courage to proceed. She ventures on once more. Ten very long minutes later, she catches sight of the concrete steps, that lead from the dirt and gravel trail to the summit of Mt. Pleasant about fifty yards away. She is breathing hard, her heart is pounding, her body damp with perspiration, and there is a throbbing pain in her side.

After she finally reaches the top of the cement stairs and the summit, she eases herself down on a rocky outcrop to catch her breath and to try to squelch her underlying fears. She scans the summit for the man she has come to meet, but just like the parking lot at the shelter house, she is alone.

Steve and his wife Beverly live in Little River, S.C.
You can contact him via www.stevenmcmillen.com.

Made in the USA
Middletown, DE
03 April 2023

27800044R00156